C000320005

Dead Again

By the same author

Come Home and be Killed
Burning is a Substitute for Loving
The Hunger in the Shadows
Nun's Castle
Ironwood
Raven's Force
Dragon's Eye
Axwater
Murder Has a Pretty Face
The Painted Castle
The Hand of Glass
Listen to the Children
Death in the Garden
Windsor Red
A Cure for Dying
Witching Murder
Footsteps in the Blood
Dead Set
Whoever Has the Heart
Baby Drop
The Morbid Kitchen
The Woman Who Was Not There
Revengeful Death
Stone Dead

Jennie Melville

Dead Again

A Charmian Daniels Mystery

MACMILLAN

First published 2000 by Macmillan
an imprint of Macmillan Publishers Ltd
25 Eccleston Place, London SW1W 9NF
Basingstoke and Oxford
Associated companies throughout the world
www.macmillan.co.uk

ISBN 0 333 76593 1

1 3 5 7 9 8 6 4 2

A CIP catalogue record for this book is available from
the British Library.

Phototypeset by Intype London Ltd
Printed and bound in Great Britain by
Mackays of Chatham plc, Chatham, Kent

Chapter One

'We have a hermit living in the shed at the bottom of our garden,' confided Birdie Peacock to Charmian Daniels, over the teacups.

'A hermit?'

'Yes, he moved in while we were away. We found him there when we got back.'

Winifred Eagle and Birdie Peacock had moved back to their small early-nineteenth-century house from the larger one in which they had started a white witchcraft and mystery bookshop when it was despoiled by dead bodies and murders. The bookshop still continued and indeed flourished, the publicity having brought in customers, but Birdie and Winifred had decided to move out.

The two friends, elderly but always well dressed with pretty jewellery, had been founder members of the White Witches of Windsor which met at irregular intervals to meditate and pray round an ancient oak in the Great Park, that old hunting ground of the Norman kings. After the meeting, if the weather permitted, they would have a picnic lunch with champagne. Charmian had been a guest once and had silently dubbed them the Champagne Witches.

Their lovely house had a large garden, the wild and

wooded end of which almost melted into the Great Park where grouse, rabbits, squirrels and deer still roamed.

'Do you mean a tramp?' asked Charmian.

'No, a hermit, someone who withdraws from the world to think, to meditate – a mystic.'

It sounded phoney to Charmian. And she noticed that Winifred, always the more cynical of the two, was keeping quiet.

'Where did he come from?'

Birdie frowned. 'He hasn't said, but he did tell me he spent a bit of time on Pinckney Heath, there's a nice little thicket there that he lived in. But it got wet.'

'That would make meditation difficult.'

Birdie gave her a cautious look, sensing irony. 'It's marshy in bits.'

Charmian nodded. She knew Pinckney Heath. Two years ago a boy and a girl had been attacked there. The boy had been badly knocked about and the girl beaten. A torch had been found but their attacker, never. A few days ago a girl had been murdered there, Felicity Harrie. An unusual name which Charmian remembered although it had not been her case.

'Are you charging him rent?'

'No, of course not.' Birdie was indignant. 'You don't make a profit out of a holy figure.'

'If you are sure he is holy.'

'You feel it,' said Birdie with conviction. 'When you see him there is an aura.'

For a moment, Charmian was silenced. Then she asked, 'How does he manage for food? Are you feeding him?'

'No,' said Birdie vaguely. 'He manages somehow.'

'Perhaps he catches a rabbit or a grouse in the Great Park,' said Winifred sardonically.

'I might give him some leftovers if I have cooked a lot of something . . .' Birdie was a very good cook ' . . . and, of course, I might throw a bone to the dog.'

'Oh, there's a dog too, is there?'

'Yes, such a nice creature with charming manners and, as you know, we left the big black cat behind in the shop to watch for mice.'

'How does the hermit manage with washing and so on?' Charmian persevered with her questions.

'That shed was fitted with plumbing, drains and electricity when my father lived here,' said Winifred. 'He was something of an astronomer and used it to watch the stars. He was always hopeful that he would see an alien force arriving.'

Charmian nodded. She had heard that Dr Eagle had been an eccentric figure. Rich, retired, well educated and mad had been the judgement passed on him by her colleague Dolly Barstow.

Charmian thought that Winifred and Birdie's hermit must have done some careful research before moving in. Except, possibly, for one thing.

'Hermits are Christians, aren't they? Do you think he will mind that you are witches?'

'White witches,' said Winifred carefully.

'White as driven snow,' admitted Charmian. 'But hardly members of the Church of England.'

'I go to communion once a year,' answered Birdie, 'and Win goes to mass.'

'Broadminded of you.'

'It is an act of courtesy,' said Birdie with dignity, 'and

once a year we invite Dr Masters and Father McKay to our service in the Great Park.'

'But do they come?'

Birdie ignored this pleasantry. 'And in any case, hermits often worship the gods of nature: the gods of the trees, the rivers, the winds.'

You had to admit, said Charmian to herself, that Birdie had quite a way with words.

There was a distant bark.

'Oh, there's Jim,' said Birdie. 'They must be back from their walk.'

'They take walks then?'

'Yes, Jim gets his walkies.'

'Hermits can go for walks, can they?'

Birdie was reproving. 'Dame Julian of Norwich, who was a famous hermit and mystic, lived in a nice little set of rooms in a garden where she received visitors. Hermits are not prisoners.'

There was another bark. Not a small dog, Charmian thought. 'Can I be taken to meet your hermit?'

Birdie led the way through the garden, which got wilder as you went through it, with a belt of trees and bushes making a barrier before the shed. The shed itself was bigger than Charmian had expected.

'This place housed my father's telescope,' said Winifred. 'I'm afraid we have always been an eccentric family.'

'Nothing eccentric in that,' observed Charmian politely. She had seen a portrait of Dr Eagle, who had looked charming, but yes, a little mad.

'Except that he was watching the skies for the Martians to arrive,' said his daughter.

Charmian absorbed this information. 'I wish I had known him.'

'He was a lovely man. A medical man, a physician. He went out to the Normandy landings with the Oxfordshires. They had a tough time – he was never the same again, my mother said. But fortunately, he had private means.'

Charmian interpreted this Edwardian phrase accurately as meaning he was rich. This too, Dolly had reported.

'Unluckily, he spent a lot of his capital preparing for the Martians. He left them a trust fund but it runs out if they don't come within the next ten years, and meanwhile Birdie and I manage.'

Birdie, too, has some of her own private means, decided Charmian. Having known her dear friends for some time now, she had long since accurately assessed their income. They were not poor. Not by any means. And then, not everyone has a trust fund coming their way, provided the Martians don't get it first.

Just then Jim the dog appeared through the bushes and stood looking at them with alert suspicion. He was a rangy, long-limbed collie with a touch of Alsatian. Intelligent and cautious but not unfriendly.

His master appeared through the trees. He was not what Charmian had expected of a hermit. He was a tall, slender man with red hair, his face shrouded in a thick beard; he was wearing dark spectacles and was dressed in neat, clean, blue jeans and a blue shirt. A gold cross hung at his throat.

The dog backed to stand protectively against his master.

'I am Charmian Daniels.' Charmian held out her

hand. 'My friends tell me you are living here in their shed.'

He nodded. 'They kindly permit it.' He had a soft, gentle voice, accentless. It was impossible to place him by it either socially or geographically. 'Nice ladies. Kind. I am resting with them.'

The unspoken implication was 'Soon I move on', but Charmian doubted it. Wondered, anyway – he was hard to read.

This was all he said and all it seemed he had to say as he turned away, his dog following him.

Charmian went back to Birdie and Winifred. 'He seems harmless enough.'

Birdie drew herself up. 'Men of God like hermits can never be called harmless. You underrate him.'

'I just meant that I don't think he is likely to murder you in your beds.'

Birdie considered this and on the whole was not pleased. 'Winifred and I were hoping that you and Sir Humphrey could come to a small party we are having next Wednesday.' She caught Winifred's eye. 'Just drinks.'

'I would like to come, but Humphrey is in America on a short visit – partly research, partly seeing his cousins.'

'Oh, dear, and you couldn't go?'

'No, too busy. You know how it is.'

'Oh, yes, of course, my dear. But I'm so glad *you* can come.'

When Charmian had gone, Winifred said, 'We are not having a party.'

'No, dear, but I wanted to find out where Humphrey was.'

'You're a wicked one,' said Winifred solemnly.

'That woman is not happy, and it's because he's not around. She's never herself when he's away.'

'Well, now we've got all the trouble of arranging a party.' But Winifred did not sound too cross.

'It's time we had one, we owe it to ourselves. And remember: you are named Witch of Title this year, it's up to you to entertain.'

When Charmian spoke to her husband on the telephone that night she said, 'You'd better come home soon or all my friends in Windsor will think you've left me.'

'You mean Birdie and Winifred.'

'Oh, they think it already. I could see Birdie studying my face and deciding I looked worried.'

'And do you?'

After a pause, Charmian said, 'There is a worry.' She knew she was on a safe, closed line that could not be tapped. 'I have received instructions . . .'

On occasion, Humphrey reflected, his dear wife did fall into jargon. What she meant by instruction was that she had been given information.

'Joan Dingham is being released for a month to live in Merrywick so that she can get used to the world outside prison and make arrangements to do a degree course at South Surrey University.'

Humphrey was silent, then he said, 'Will she be safe?'

'My job is to keep her safe.'

Joan Dingham was the most hated child murderer of the last three decades. Four children had been beaten, strangled and buried in boxes. The media had called her

'The Silent Killer' because after confessing her guilt, she never again spoke of it.

Charmian had insisted on having the detailed police files and photographs of the murders. She wanted to know everything there was to know. Not pretty reading. Four girls, in pairs, all killed within a few weeks of each other.

There had also been an earlier murder, a singleton, with some resemblance to the Dingham killings but the police never managed to tie it in. Still, it was there, on record, unsolved.

'I can see she must be well hated. Can't be many people who would want to be friends with a woman like that.'

That was innocent of Humphrey, Charmian thought, because the woman did have what she called friends. Charmian had been given the list:

Madge Fisher, school teacher, she had been a prison visitor.

Margie Wells, a librarian, who ran the prison library while serving her own sentence for fraud and reported that Joan had good taste in books.

Jeanie Bott, an old school chum, who still kept up with her. (Here Charmian had made a note that Jeanie was also a friend, or anyway knew, Beryl Andrea Barker, aka Baby.)

Three friends – not bad for a multiple killer.

Joan Dingham also had a sister, Lulu, or Lou, and a son, Pip, both of whom visited her and wrote her letters.

'She's got her circle,' said Charmian, assessing the situation. She knew that even to these few Joan never spoke about the killings, although it was believed that she did talk to her sister. She had to have someone,

Charmian thought. 'And I suppose I will have to keep an eye on them. In a case like this, you can't count on anyone's real motives and sympathies.'

'Why you?'

Charmian shrugged. 'I am trusted. Even the Castle trusts me.'

Humphrey acknowledged that his wife was successful and the Southern Register Documentation and Crime unit (SRADIC), which had been created for her nominally to collect, register and record all the documents of crime within the South Downs area, had been a powerful instrument in her hands. It gave her the means to check and interfere. She also had two excellent deputies in Inspector Dolly Barstow and the enigmatic Inspector George Rewley.

'I suppose she will be using another name when she gets out?'

'Maybe – even I don't know that yet. She may insist on using her own. She looks different now, of course. And she will be bringing a minder from the prison.'

'How long has she been inside?'

'Twenty years.'

A lot of murders in those twenty years, including Pinckney Heath where Felicity Harrie's hand had been cut with the shape of a cross.

'Things have changed outside. She'll never cope.'

'They say she's as tough as old boots,' said Charmian gloomily. 'She'd have to be.'

'How many people have promised to kill her if she ever sets foot outside her prison cell?'

Charmian did not answer. 'There's been plenty of talk,' she said eventually. 'It's hard to know your friends from your enemies in a case like this. I mean she's said to have friends, but who knows if they are really friends?'

'Never mind,' said Humphrey. 'I'll be home soon. I'll see she doesn't get killed.'

Charmian was somewhat reassured, but she could not help wondering if the arrival of the hermit had not got something to do with the expected release of Joan Dingham.

But how could that be so?

And was he friend or enemy? Or someone who might secretly have signed a big contract for a book on her and was writing it all up?

You can become very suspicious, Charmian found, dealing with a case like this one.

When Charmian went to have her hair done at the hairdressers at the bottom of Peascod Street where Baby – Beryl Andrea Barker, retired criminal – held sway, she was surprised to hear Baby say, 'So when is Joanie arriving?'

Charmian, head bent back over the basin as her hair was being washed, kept silent.

'Oh, come on, I know and you know. Joanie is on her way. A little outing for a good girl.'

Charmian gave in. 'How do you know?'

'Spent a month in the same nick, didn't we, before I was moved on. I still keep in touch with some of my friends from there. Not her, though. She could be a surly cow.'

'Really?'

'Although charming when she chose.' Baby applied herself to the rinse. 'Never spoke about the murders, except the odd hint that she was put up to it by her partner, and that she herself was innocent. There were two of them in it, you know, and people wondered about a third.'

'I did hear it said.'

'Of course, we all know that in affairs of that sort, one partner in crime always blames the other. And who knows? Maybe it's true.' Baby studied Charmian's face. 'They never caught the other one – she killed herself first.'

'I only know what I've read and been told.'

'I bet you've got some thoughts on it, though. I always thought it was Lou, the other sister, naughty of me.'

'Enough of all that. How are you?' said Charmian, changing the subject. 'I must say the salon looks splendid since you've had it redone. Did you use Mr Duckett?' This was the man who Charmian had recommended.

'No, he turned out to be a mite expensive for a little hairdresser like me. No, John Chappell did it for me: rewired, repainted, helped with the colour scheme. He has very good taste. He's got his own firm, Castle Decor, he calls it.'

And attractive to women, was Charmian's interpretation, whereas Mr Duckett was fat and bald, a much married man whose wife did the accounts.

'Has he worked for the Castle?'

'I believe he did something, but not for the royal apartments.'

Charmian knew that if the Castle could use local firms they did.

Baby swept a comb through Charmian's hair. 'Not

bad days for me really, although I'm glad I've put all that behind me.' Crime, she meant.

'Pleased to hear it,' said Charmian, face muffled in a towel. She was never quite sure how much she believed in Baby's virtue: a movable feast, she was inclined to think.

'I've opened another salon, did you know?' Baby got her tongue round the word salon with pleasure. She was enjoying her success.

'Where?'

'In Slough. I know it's not fashionable but it's where the money is.'

'I admire you. Baby, I truly do. Congratulations. You must have done very well here financially.'

Baby gave a discreet smile. 'I've managed. I'm a saver.'

You must be, thought Charmian, I hope you haven't robbed a bank. But all she said aloud was, 'When you open your next salon, in Knightsbridge, say opposite Harvey Nicols, I will be your first customer.'

Baby laughed. 'Do you think I will ever do that? Well, if I do, you will get your first visit for free.'

Baby combed Charmian's hair. 'Your tint could do with a touch up . . . Just to brighten it a little.'

'No.' Charmian never admitted to the tinted shampoo she applied in the privacy of her own bathroom.

They were both silent for a minute, thinking about Joan Dingham. Then Baby said, 'Her sister still lives here.'

Charmian nodded. 'I know that.' The sister had been mentioned in the police dossier.

'She's younger than Joan, but not much. Lou called herself Joan's best friend, and I guess she was. I think she was shocked at what came out at the trial, but she always blamed Joan's partner, Rhos, more than her sister, and she thought there was someone else besides, but that was just fancy. Of course, Rhos had the good sense to do herself in before the police arrived on the scene. Joan never mentioned Rhos but she talked about Lou a lot. There's feeling on both sides.'

Baby started to dry Charmian's hair. 'I'm giving you a bit of a bounce on the crown, suits you.'

Charmian agreed that it did suit her, but she was not thinking about her looks at the moment and did not really want to discuss her appearance.

They did not talk for a bit then, as Charmian was paying her bill, Baby said, 'She's risking something coming out of prison, she's safe there. The kid's mother – the murder she was not charged with – is bound to have a go at her. And if she doesn't, someone else will.'

'She'll be looked after,' replied Charmian. 'She might not use her own name and no one will know where she will be living.'

'Think so?' Baby helped Charmian on with her coat. The salon was nearly empty. 'It'll get out and you know it will.'

They were both thinking of Diana. Diana belonged to that group of female criminals from Baby's past. She had been a powerful if criminous influence on Baby, but a certain inner canniness had brought Baby back to the straight and narrow and interestingly into hair-dressing, which had been Diana's profession. Or, at least, her legal one. She had had a secret life, all right. All Diana's secrets – where she kept her money, the house she had in Malta under another name, even the hint that she had had a child – had begun to emerge when she went to prison and fell ill. She had once been said to be dying of cancer, but she was a survivor. In a way, she would never die, and Baby knew this as much as anyone. Diana still influenced her life.

'It's a dangerous game being a killer,' said Charmian.

'That's not your sort of joke.'

'I wasn't joking.' Charmian's own relationship with Diana had been complicated. She had known her in those earlier days.

'Want a spray?' Baby held out a shiny tin.

'Yes.' As Charmian bent her head she frowned. 'Do you keep up with the others?' Others in the gang, she meant. 'Bee and Phil?'

'No, and you know I don't. Once I decided to go respectable I had to cut them out . . . I send a card at Christmas and I did Bee's hair for her once when she popped in, but otherwise nothing.'

They were still in touch then, whatever she said. Charmian made a mental note.

'I thought I saw Bee walking down Peascod Street last week.'

'You might have done.' Baby was vague. 'It was Di who held us together.'

Charmian nodded. I bet if I tapped your phone, she told herself, I'd hear something interesting.

'Do you know anything about hermits? There's one come to live in the town.'

'No,' said Baby, crisply. 'Hermits don't come to me to get their hair cut.'

Her attention was diverted by the arrival of a delivery van from Fortnum and Mason.

*

Charmian extricated her car from the car park at the back of the salon which was somewhat more crowded than usual, and drove home without another word being said to Baby. Sometimes, she told herself, she would like to stamp on Baby's confident, pretty face, and scream. Charmian liked Beryl Andrea Barker, she was attractive, lively and a good hairdresser. In many ways, she admired her, but it was almost impossible to know her without suspecting her. Of something, of anything.

Baby was on the phone as soon as Charmian had disappeared. 'Bee, thank goodness you're there.'

'Thought I told you not to telephone.'

'I'm nervous. I really am. Bee. Is Phil there?'

'No, she's not back yet.' Bee kicked Phil's ankle while mouthing 'shut up'. 'And there's no need to be nervous. Being a good girl for too long has weakened your nerves.'

'It's Joan coming out . . . joining us . . . she'd terrify anyone.' A pause, then Baby said, 'And you know what we always said: once she's out you can count on a couple of kids being done in, just to celebrate.'

'That was just a joke.'

'Yeah, sure. One of those jokes you don't laugh at. She always hinted she was just one of a group. She called the others her little friends.'

'I thought she didn't speak about it.'

'Not seriously. She made jokes, you know, take it how you would, she wasn't quite mute.' A pause before Baby went back to her worries. 'And Diana. She's still around, you know. The undead.' A kind of ghost from the past who they all remembered.

'Don't use that name,' commanded Bee harshly.

'No, I won't, I haven't. Not in public, anyway, only among us.' She had always admired Diana. Well, they all had. 'She'd be forty, you know.' Older really, but forty officially.

'I do know,' said Bee harshly, being still older.

'I said I'd put on a little do for Joan,' said Baby.

'Order the champagne, then, we'll make it a do, but don't use the word celebration, you've put me right off it.'

Images of dead girls killed in 'celebration' of Joan Dingham's release were powerful.

'I've already ordered the champagne. Vintage. Joan likes the good stuff.' They all did.

Baby had one other worry.

'The girls here tell me this man turned up . . . God knows who he is. Prowling round. Asking questions. I didn't see him myself. He's got a dog, too.'

In the next few days Charmian had several meetings about Joan Dingham's arrival.

First, she had a talk with her local colleagues, Inspector Parker and Sergeant Emily Agent who would be responsible for Joan's safety.

'She insists on using her own name, so there's no question of her hiding.' John Parker was a tall, thin man, young for his rank. 'Probably wise. She'd certainly be sussed out.'

'She hasn't changed very much,' said Emily Agent. 'And you can't hide that nose.'

Charmian nodded. 'She wasn't bad-looking.'

'I'm not saying she wasn't. And she isn't now. But it's a Roman nose, isn't it? Like the Duke of Wellington.'

'Anyway, she's coming as herself, loud and clear. So that makes our job more difficult, but we shall keep someone with her at all times. It's expensive, but there you are, it's better than what might happen.'

'So who will it be?' asked Charmian.

'Me.' Emily smiled. 'Or most of the time, at any rate. It has to be a woman for obvious reasons, and I'm not married – I don't even have a boyfriend at the moment. I shall have someone else to relieve me on occasion and then, as John says, it's only for a matter of weeks.'

'Of course, the university people are fussing a bit. You've seen them, I suppose?'

'I'm going on there now,' said Charmian. 'I've got an appointment with Dr Greenham. He's arranging the work side of things. Joan will work on her own and have a special room in the university library. She will go to a few lectures if things work out. They have video links and such like.'

'Just as well,' said Inspector Parker, 'she could do the whole thing that way, all private and on her own. But no, the powers that be think this must be tried.'

'I have some sympathy with that,' said Charmian. 'Provided she knows the risks she's walking into.'

'Wants to try them, I think.' Emily Agent had seen more of Joan Dingham recently than the other two. Charmian had only met the woman once, and then briefly. She found it hard to assess what impression the woman had made on her, it was as if a glass wall had come down between them so that you could see and hear but not touch.

The glass wall was called prejudice, she supposed.

'If anything happens to her, then it's our heads on the block,' said John Parker gloomily.

Dr Greenham had met Charmian at the big main entrance to the university buildings. 'Easy to get lost in this rabbit warren,' he explained easily. 'Come along to the Common Room and have a drink while we talk. Wouldn't dare let you see my room, it's awash with papers and books. I'm external examiner for a university you've probably never heard of.'

Dr Greenham was neatly dressed, with a sharp hair cut and an easy manner.

'So she wants to do a degree in sociology,' he said.

'Can she do that?'

'She's probably as capable of it as anyone else. She'll have to go through a general first year course leading into it and by then she may have decided not to go ahead with it. They often do.'

'Really?' Charmian was surprised. In her day, you went on from where you had started.

'It's not a soft option although it looks it,' said Greenham. 'I'll give her a reading list, show her round the library, and introduce her to one or two fellow students.' He sounded pleasant but detached. He was a smooth young man and meant to go on being smooth. 'If in trouble, may I call on you?' It wasn't quite a question, he just meant Charmian to know that trouble was not his business. 'And if I fall into any kind of trouble, I shall hold you to account.'

'You won't,' Charmian assured him, although honestly, who knew?

'She's not the most popular of women.'

'She'll have a kind of minder,' Charmian said.

'Like royalty – the Princess of Crime, the Queen of Murder.'

Charmian did not answer: the woman had to be protected, it was just a job.

But she felt gloomy as if several unpleasant responsibilities were hanging over her like birds of prey, beaks at the ready.

Joan Dingham travelled with a kind of entourage: a prison officer and a police officer, both in plain clothes, but both looking as if they had just left the army. They were not exactly friendly travelling companions because you couldn't quite trust them. She had taken pains to get on well with them, such as they were. No sense in queering your own pitch.

Two friends – yes, she had friends, she told herself – had got on the train at Reading. Madge and Jeanie. Had made quite a fuss of her. Margie Wells, the prison librarian, a really close friend, Joan told herself, was not out yet. Soon. Another month.

Joan herself was dressed neatly and with some style. This had always been her mark and she saw no reason why prison should change this. It was easy enough to order clothes by post or phone and if some famous stores were surprised at the address the goods were to go to, it didn't stop the orders arriving, and the bills were paid. Looks counted. She was a famous woman, she would be observed.

Hair was a different matter and she would be glad of some good professional advice. She had changed the colour several times but home jobs (or prison jobs more accurately because she hoped she would never think of a cell as home) showed. You could always tell. Some subtlety was missing.

Lou joined the train at Windsor and all the friends gathered quietly in Joan's carriage. She travelled first class, of course, so they could talk and make plans.

Lou reached across to take Joan's hand. 'I love you, Joanie.'

Joan pressed her sister's hand. 'Love you too.'

'You're the best sister anyone ever had.'

'Sisters help each other, Lou.'

They smiled at each other, one of those close smiles that says a lot if you already know the answer.

'I know that school was important,' said Lou. 'It was where you got to know Rhos.'

No one was allowed to talk about Rhos, only Lou ventured to do so.

'My best school mate,' said Joan slowly. Bar one, really, but she did not say this aloud.

'St Edyth's School,' went on Lou. 'Long since gone. Part of a big comprehensive now.'

The train sped on. One of the party produced a bottle of champagne and some plastic cups. There was enough for a couple of drinks each, excluding the minders.

'I must get to the hairdresser,' said Joan, passing her hand over her head. 'Colour's all wrong.'

Her sister appraised it. 'Could do with a touch of something.'

'Your hair looks good. Where do you go?'

'Where do you think? I go to Baby.'

'Right. Beryl Andrea Barker, here I come.'

'I've met a very nice couple of witches in Windsor,' said Lou conversationally.

'Oh really?'

'White witches. They run a bookshop – Crime and Witches. You meet interesting people there.'

'I bet you do. I must look in.'

'You'll be a draw.'

'Not sure if I want to be,' said Joan modestly.

There was a pause. Lou lowered her voice so the minders could not hear. 'I ought to tell you that you are not the only famous face coming back to town.'

'I heard about that,' said Joan cautiously.

'Baby told me. She'll tell you.'

'Di, is it? I heard she was dead.'

'So did I. She may be a sort of ghost.'

'Is she coming to the party?'

'Yes.'

'You never could keep Di away from a party,' said Joan. 'Alive or dead. Years since we met. I may not know her whatever her condition.'

'She'll know you,' said Lou uneasily. 'Know me too, I expect.'

Humphrey returned home that evening, and when they had kissed, he said, 'What's up with your friends, the white witches? As I drove home, I passed one of them – Birdie, I think it was – and she was hurrying through the streets looking distressed. I leant out of the car and tried to talk to her but she disappeared down the road in the direction of the Great Park without a word. In fact, I don't think she noticed me.'

Charmian poured them some wine. She took a good draught herself.

'I won't say she was talking to herself and pulling her hair.'

'I should think not,' said Charmian indignantly.

'But it looked like it.'

'I will ring them after we've eaten.'

But she didn't get a chance.

Only a few minutes later, while she was mixing the salad. Birdie herself telephoned. Her voice was shaky. 'Could you come to see us?'

'Yes, sure, what is it?'

'It's our hermit. He's disappeared.'

Charmian looked at her husband, he nodded and mouthed that he had told her so. He had known there was trouble. Charmian sighed. 'It'll have to be later this evening.'

Nervously, Birdie said, 'Do you think Humphrey would come? A man's judgement, you know . . .'

Charmian swallowed her feminist fury. When she thought of things she had heard Birdie say about warlocks . . . 'Yes, I think he might.'

Humphrey, just that day back from a course on theatre studies in New York ('I know I can't act,' he had said, 'and I will never write for the theatre, but I do like thinking about it.'), followed by a quick trip to the Manhattan Theater Troupe, seized with quiet pleasure on this piece of real-life drama.

'You've changed,' she said as they walked to where Birdie and Winifred lived. 'I don't know whether it's my influence or whether it's because you have ceased being a courtier.' But has he? Do they ever, she thought?

'I've changed all by myself.' Humphrey was probably laughing at her.

Birdie and Winifred both came to the door to meet them. They must have been awaiting them keenly, probably looking out of the upper window that commanded a view of the curve in the street. Both were wearing lollipop-coloured, loose silk dresses, and had bare feet. Different lollipops though. Birdie wore peppermint green while Winifred wore raspberry pink. Charmian recognized the silks as what she called their stop and go costumes, worn only in times of stress. Clearly this was one such time.

She gave each of them a hug since this seemed to be the required therapy. 'So he's gone. But why the panic? I expect he's just moved on, he was probably that sort.'

Birdie shook her head. 'No, you mustn't talk of "that sort", people are never just "that sort". It's not worthy of you to say so.'

'Quite right,' said Humphrey, showing the masculine judgement for which he had been brought here. 'Birdie knows what she's talking about.'

'Indeed I do, we have had wanderers stay in the garden before now. We are on their route and they always give an indication before moving on. Unconsciously even, but we can read them . . . A tidy up here, a little bonfire there, sometimes a small theft from the kitchen – nothing of value, but we know what it means. And it might equally be a small offering to us.'

'You're a good woman,' said Humphrey with genuine admiration.

Birdie shook her head. 'But not this time, and he

was a hermit, a holy man, not a wanderer. Wanderers,' she added sadly, 'are rarely if ever holy.'

Charmian noted that all this time Winifred had been silent, and she remembered thinking that Win had not felt the holiness of their hermit as fervently as had Birdie. She might not have believed in it at all.

'What do you want me to do?'

Winifred spoke then, 'She wants you to find him.'

Charmian swung round to look at Birdie. 'But what is worrying you? He is a big strong fellow, perfectly capable of taking care of himself.'

There was a bark.

'He's left the dog.' Birdie was very nervous.

Another bark. 'He's down in the garden,' said Winifred. 'Right at the end. Won't come in.'

Charmian looked at Humphrey. 'That is a bit odd,' he said. 'Let's have a look.'

The dog barked again. As they approached, he growled.

'He's guarding something,' said Birdie. She was good on animal noises.

Charmian looked at what lay between the dog's feet.

It was a hand, a bloodstained hand.

Chapter Two

Charmian stared at the hand, then she put out a foot to touch it delicately. The dog growled, but in a muted way, and made no effort to attack Charmian.

'Oh, be careful,' breathed Birdie. Her voice trembled. She still did not like the way the dog growled. It was a warning.

'Watch yourself, Birdie,' commanded Winifred. 'You know blood makes you faint.'

'I can't bear to look.' She did look, though, peeping through her fingers.

Winifred put her arm round her friend while looking pleadingly at Humphrey. He hurried forward to support Birdie.

'Don't worry,' said Charmian crisply. 'Can't you see? It's not a real hand.' She poked it again with her foot. 'It's china. A good facsimile. Well done. A model used to promote nail varnish, I should think.'

There was a moment of silence.

'The blood,' said Birdie.

'That may be real.' The hand was a bit earth stained also, and the earth was certainly real.

'Are you telling us the hermit had a false hand?' Winifred's tone was firm.

Birdie moaned. 'No, no, I'd have noticed. I am not

entirely stupid. And you would have noticed. Think of all the St John's Ambulance work we have both done. We would know a false hand.'

The picture of Birdie and Winifred acting as emergency nurses although unexpected to Charmian was also convincing: they were capable ladies.

'You used to do Ascot, didn't you? I saw you there once or twice,' put in Humphrey.

'Yes, and the Notting Hill Carnival and also Covent Garden on occasion, but only to oblige – we don't care for opera.' This was Winifred. 'We haven't done much lately with the bookshop taking off so well and the white witches keeping us busy. And, of course, maintaining the shed . . . well, we kept it tidy at least.' She looked at Birdie for support who stretched out her hand to her friend.

Not usual in their relationship, Winifred is usually the bossy, strong one, Charmian observed to herself, so what's up?

Winifred took a deep breath, then said, 'My father died there, one night, when the moon was full. So it has always been kept as something of a holy place.'

'Haunted even, you know,' observed Birdie.

'There has been a sense of habitation,' said Winifred hesitantly. 'Perhaps by Papa and his friends, perhaps not.'

Birdie nodded at her friend. 'We thought that the shed was used by . . .' she hesitated. 'Other than the usual wandering visitors, just occasional travelling visitors, you know, and we respected their privacy. Just as we did Dr Eagle's.'

'I am sorry,' said Humphrey. 'I knew Dr Eagle, of course. I am sorry he had such a lonely death.'

'Not quite alone,' said Winifred sadly, 'there was a lady with him when he died. No one knew but us, and she had gone by the time we found him.'

'She sent flowers to the funeral, though,' Birdie hurried to say. 'With love from Lady Mary.'

'Although what sort of a lady,' said Winifred, even more sadly, 'we never knew.'

Humphrey was silent. Well, good luck to the late Dr Eagle, he was thinking. Wouldn't mind going that way myself. He kept his eyes away from his wife, however, Charmian was good at reading his thoughts.

Then he found he could read hers at this minute and he didn't like what he read.

'There's something else,' said Charmian. 'Take a closer look . . . It's a woman's hand.'

Without waiting for them to say anything, she advanced towards the shed where the hermit had taken up his quarters. The dog let her pass. Whatever orders he had been given it did not include keeping visitors out of the hut.

Inside it was tidy. A sleeping bag lay across a simple camp bed. A table set out with a looking glass was in one corner, a washbasin and a flush lavatory in the other. The floor was unpolished wood. Light poured through the great window in the roof. It was simple but comfortable enough.

'Papa used to sleep down here when he was watching the skies,' said Winifred. 'Didn't want to miss anything.' She sounded neutral on the subject of the Martians or any aliens. Ladies were different, no neutrality there. Winifred coughed. 'I have a small confession to make: I did just take a tiny look round when the hermit was out . . . well, we are two women on our own . . . And I found a card with Dr Harrie written on it. The hermit's name, I think. It interested me.'

'Dr Harrie?' Humphrey was frowning. 'I knew a Harrie once, he wasn't a doctor then. Unusual name, though.'

The hermit had hung a loose rough tweed overcoat on a peg on the wall. Along this wall, which was opposite the bed, was a shelf with several small books on it. Underneath was a water bowl for the dog, and a length of rug for him to sleep on.

The dog came in carrying the hand, and settled down on his rug. Not to sleep however, his eyes remained alert.

'I think the hand is his toy,' said Charmian, regretfully. 'He seemed such a nice dog, too.'

There was a noise outside, just a cough and a footfall.

Humphrey was the first to speak.

'Good evening, Dr Harrie.' He held out his hand. 'Humphrey Kent. Weren't we at school together?'

The hermit said nothing, staring at Humphrey. Then he nodded. 'Humphrey Kent? Didn't know you at first. We've both changed.' He turned to Charmian, studying her face carefully. 'I know you, ma'am.'

'My wife,' Humphrey murmured.

Harrie bowed to Charmian. 'And you are also the distinguished policewoman. I am Dr Harrie.'

Birdie and Winifred had been watching silently. Now Winifred said bluntly, 'Why are you going round like this?'

Dr Harrie looked down at his clothes.

'Pretending to be a hermit and living in our garden?' This time it was Birdie who spoke.

'I wasn't pretending. I have been living on my own, speaking to no one and living like a hermit for some months.'

'At Pinckney Heath?' This time it was Charmian.

'Yes. I had a purpose. My granddaughter, Felicity, was found murdered there. I thought I might find her killer.'

It had not been Charmian's case, but she knew the name. 'The Harrie girl was your grandchild?'

He nodded. 'I wanted to find out who killed her. The police didn't seem to be doing much good.'

'They haven't given up,' said Charmian.

'I thought if I hung around Pinckney Heath like a tramp . . . I thought I might find something, see something. Or perhaps someone would speak to me. Let out something that I could hang on to.'

'And did you?'

Slowly he said no, he hadn't, but Charmian thought his expression was interesting. 'So why did you come here?' asked Birdie. 'How did you know where to come? A hermit might have heard about it, but you aren't a real hermit.'

'I knew Dr Eagle.' He turned to Winifred. 'I worked for him once or twice for a few months. He brought me here once and we spent a night studying the heavens.'

'I don't remember you coming,' said Winifred, her tone was sceptical.

'You were away at school. But your mother was here. Betty.'

Winifred nodded. Betty had been her mother's name. Slowly, reluctantly, she was beginning to believe him.

'So you decided to take refuge here? Why?'

'I remembered its atmosphere of peace. Also, of course, I did not think you were living here now. I believed you had moved away and the house was empty.'

'We did move away. We opened a bookshop where we lived for a short while before moving back here.' Because of two bodies in the garden. Nothing to do with us, of course, but we felt happier back here. But she did not say this aloud.

'Did you call yourself a hermit?' asked Birdie. 'Or was it the ladies?'

He smiled at her, a gentle smile. 'I have been a sort of hermit since my wife died.' He added, 'The murder of my granddaughter made things worse: my son had died leaving her with only a mother. Alison has gone to live in Canada. Can't blame her.'

'Why did you leave Pinckney Heath?' Charmian asked.

'I had to move on. It's a public park, even the wildish bit where I was dossing down, and after a bit I was noticed.' He paused. 'I thought it best, in the circumstances, to leave. I shall have to get in touch with the police.'

'What do you mean?' Charmian demanded. She was beginning to wonder about the sanity of this fellow.

The dog appeared, he was still carrying the hand in his mouth.

'You've seen the hand, of course.'

'Yes,' said Charmian, 'it seems to be the sort of thing you see in a beautician's salon or something like that. Hairdresser's maybe.' She found herself remembering Baby's establishment. 'The nails are very pretty.' Each one was painted a different colour.

She still didn't know what to make of the apparent blood.

'Where did the dog find it?' she asked.

'He dug it up.'

'Where did he dig?'

There was silence then he said, 'I am not sure; he came back with it in his mouth.'

'But you know where you were, where he was likely to have been digging?'

Dr Harrie said that he had been wandering for some days, thinking about life and death. He was not quite sure where he had been. The Great Park, you know, was large and wild. 'And of course, the dog ranged far and wide.'

He knows pretty exactly, I am sure, thought the knowledgeable Charmian. And I shall find out. He is not a good liar, not enough practise, I suspect, and perhaps not really trying either.

She looked down at the hand which the dog was snuffling at. 'He finds it interesting.'

'It smells of death,' said Dr Harrie.

Charmian's mobile phone and pager were always with her and, at this moment, the phone rang in her bag.

To her surprise, it was Inspector Dolly Barstow. 'Dolly . . . I thought you were away.'

'No, back,' said Dolly tersely, 'holiday complete frost.' Charmian suspected this meant a quarrel with her current young man – not all that young either – he was a high-ranking, married, police officer from the Met with two marriages already behind him. Met his match in Dolly, though, no doubt. 'Just as well.'

'Oh?' No need to say more, Dolly was going to tell

her. Charmian moved to the door of the hut, leaving her husband, Birdie and Winifred to talk to Dr Harrie. Tether him too, they weren't going to let him get away.

'A girl's body has been found on a bit of rough ground close to Threadneedle Alley. She's been strangled. Possibly raped as well. Anyway, damage to the vaginal area.'

Charmian was surprised. 'I'm not involved in a local case like that, Dolly. Doesn't concern SRADIC, goes to the local CID boys. You know that. Why have you been called?'

'You'll want to see this one.' Dolly had an unusually clear and carrying voice.

Out of the corner of her eye, Charmian could see that she had an attentive audience in the four in the hut. Humphrey was preserving the most discretion but then he had had the most practice.

'It seems likely the victim is Dr Greenham's daughter. Remember him? He's on his way down from Ascot where he lives. If you hurry you will be here before him.' Dolly added, in a quieter tone of voice, 'And of course the local boys are here. In some numbers. Likewise the press. Parker's here too. He called me. Bit wary of calling you.'

'I don't bite.'

Don't you just, she could almost read Dolly's thoughts.

'I am on my way.'

She turned to face her expectant audience. Even the dog was looking at her.

'I have to go, I am afraid.'

Humphrey spoke up at once. 'Shall I drive you?'

'No, I can call a police car. And, anyway, I don't know when I'll be back.'

'One of those, eh?'

'Might be. But I'll try to keep it short.'

Dolly Barstow was waiting for her. By her side stood Inspector Parker.

Parker muttered that Chief Inspector Webley had just arrived and Inspector Round, also of the local CID, was following. 'Been at some CID binge,' was his comment. The two officers, close friends and rivals, had been drinking with friends in the Willow Tree pub on the Oxford road when the message got through along with word of what Webley called 'SRADIC's sticky fingers' already being attached to the case.

'You can't ignore her, Ron,' Chief Inspector Webley had said to Round. 'Charmian's got influence and she sits in the middle of everything and knows everything. Probably knows more about you than you do yourself.'

'Not much about me to know,' said Ron Round, much married and famously faithful to a working wife, also CID.

'You're lucky,' muttered Webley, whose case was different.

Charmian knew both Webley and Round and knew that, as she both outranked them and was a woman, she was not popular with them. But she had learnt to work with them.

She nodded at Parker. 'I know them. Now show me the body.'

Across from them, the usual dejected-looking young figure stood by a canvas-shrouded form. First year detective constables always got the worst jobs, and no one liked standing guard by a dead body, especially if it was a child, and especially if they had seen what it looked like first.

There was also, as Dolly had said, a growing group of reporters to whom a television crew had been added. Uniformed constables were keeping them back behind the cordoned off area. There were also onlookers: locals come to see what the trouble was.

It was a scrubby bit of land with some shrubs and a desolate trio of small trees. It was destined to be developed into a small shopping centre, but litigation of one sort or another had stayed the developers' hand.

Two young people, presumably those who had found the body, were standing together. Amy Fraser and Peter Robb.

'That's Miss Daniels, Lady Whatsername,' whispered Peter to Amy. 'I deliver the papers there, it's my weekend job.'

Amy stared. 'Do you think she knows us?'

'Might do, if she looks. She hasn't looked.'

'I wish we'd just gone away and let someone else find the body.'

Peter wished this himself, but unlike his companion, he had a conscience and a sense of duty.

Amy answered his unspoken question, 'My dad says when in trouble, say nothing.' Her father was a distinguished barrister.

'If you can manage it,' returned Peter. 'My dad says, run!' His father had started out driving a bus and now owned a fleet.

The pair looked at each other. It so happened that both sets of parents, being friends, were on a Nile cruise together and out of touch.

'Has your father ever run?' asked Amy.

'Several times, I should think,' said Peter. 'But I don't believe your pa has ever been silent.'

They grinned at each other. If ever they did marry, and the matter had come up once or twice lately, then it would be a good match, but Amy had to get Cambridge over first. And it was a long haul to becoming a brain surgeon.

Charmian made her way across to where the dead girl lay. The detective constable saluted. 'DC Bob Dodd, ma'am.' He knew Charmian.

'Let me have a look, please.'

Bob Dodd peeled back the canvas from the head, wishing he could drag his eyes away.

A young girl with pretty dark hair, and a much made-up face, with heavy eyeshadow, lashes melded together into clumps with mascara and thick red lipstick. A very young girl for all the make-up, thirteen or fourteen at most. The mascara had run down her face, perhaps she had been crying. There was a great blue bruise on her forehead and down one cheek. The right eye had been hit, so that there was blood, and Charmian thought she saw the gleam of bone.

'Show me the rest,' she ordered.

Slowly young Dodd rolled back the covering, and then she understood his reluctance.

Not what you'd want to see twice.

Her jeans were drawn down to her ankles, the underpants torn, bloodstained and muddy. That was bad enough, but the thighs and lower abdomen were bruised and bloody and torn too.

Ravaged, that was the word.

Charmian leant forward to help the young constable cover up the girl. Neither of them spoke.

For a moment she stood there silently, then she walked up to where the two inspectors stood.

'The police surgeon has seen her and pronounced her dead,' said Dolly, 'and the pathologist and forensics are on their way.' She turned her head as a plain black van and a car arrived. 'In fact, that's them now.'

'How do you know it's the Greenham girl?'

'We found an envelope addressed to her, Fiona Greenham, in the pocket of the jeans.'

'She's loaded with make-up, more than I would have expected.'

Parker shrugged. 'They all do it. Family probably don't know she has the stuff. Most likely she keeps it hidden and puts it on when she goes out.' He had a young daughter himself and had often felt like conducting an inspection when she went out, but he had never been able to bring himself to do it.

'There's Dr Greenham. I told him to come to the hospital, not here,' said Dolly. 'You stay here, I'll greet him and bring him over.' Or keep him back, if she could.

He didn't need bringing over, however, and he was with them in a rush, leaving Dolly behind.

'What is all this? Where is she?'

'If you'd let me take you to the hospital, you could wait there,' said Dolly quickly as she caught up with him.

'No, bloody way.' And he strode across the grass to the covered bundle. Before she could stop him he was drawing the cloth back from the girl's face.

He stood in silence, then covered his face with his hands.

Charmian walked up to him and put her hand on his arm. He spun round at once.

'That is not my daughter. She is nothing like my daughter. I don't know what poor girl you have there but it is not Fiona. She is not my child.' Then his grief and shock turned to anger. 'And I think you owe me an explanation as to why you thought she was.'

'You're sure that this is not your daughter?' Violent death could change the appearance.

'Of course, I am sure. Do you think I don't know my own child?' He rounded on her fiercely. 'I could hit you for that . . . But no, no, it is not Fiona. This girl is, more heavily built, coarser.'

But still dead, Charmian thought. He could have used a prettier word than coarse. 'Come and sit in the car.'

'I bloody won't. If I get in any car, it will be my own car and I will drive home. And I may see my solicitor. I may sue for damages.'

'In the girl's pocket was an envelope addressed to Miss Fiona Greenham.'

'She was writing to my daughter then.' He was still angry. 'Hadn't posted the letter.'

'It was franked,' pointed out Charmian. 'We'd better see your daughter, hadn't we? She may know who this girl is.'

'I won't let her see this,' said Frank Greenham vehemently.

'No, we won't ask that of her, we'll find a way round it.' Charmian spoke gently but she was lying and she knew it. Fiona might have to see the dead girl. 'Where is Fiona?'

But of course, he did not know.

Where was she?

*

Frank Greenham had met on his doorstep the policeman who had come to deliver the message, the warning even, about the dead girl. At that time, Frank had only just discovered that Fiona had been out all day and was not yet home. No sign of her having been back to the house either.

His wife, Deirdre, without tears because the girl's thoughtlessness made her angry, had admitted that she had reason to believe that Fiona had not spent the night at home. Deirdre was Greenham's second wife (third, fourth or fifth love, they stacked up) and she was not a natural mother. She liked the girl for being pretty and clever (her father's daughter), but she showed signs of promiscuity (her father's daughter again), and Deirdre jibbed at having to take responsibility for this too. But the damn thing was she was fond of the girl; underneath the make-up was a friendly child. To think of her as dead was hard to take in. Murdered, too, possibly. She had wanted to go with Frank to the hospital where he had expected to find the body, but he wouldn't let her come with him.

'Too much for you, couldn't let you do it,' he had said. But that was not the reason she discovered: he had found out where the body still lay, on a patch of rough ground in the heart of Windsor, and intended to go there and force his way through to get sight of the body and the place.

Deirdre would have been in the way.

Never underrate the investigative powers of an experienced academic, she told herself as she watched him drive away. They are trained to ask questions which draw out the right answers. And they network, so they always know whom to ask. She thought Frank had probably got hold of the top journalist on the *Windsor Whistler*. Eddy would be wherever the body was.

Frank was still away, when the door opened and banged in a manner used only by Fiona. Deirdre stood still in the kitchen, a shiver running up her back and down her arms.

Do ghosts bang doors?

Fiona opened the kitchen door and called out 'Deirdre? Here's the wanderer back,' as her stepmother fell to the ground.

Fiona rushed over. 'Dee, why have you fainted? You're not pregnant, are you? Are you in the club? That'd make two of us.'

Dr Frank Greenham returned home later than he would have wished, having been held back to make a statement – one of non recognition, eh? he had enquired savagely – and now, in company of Charmian Daniels, he found his wife and his daughter sitting in the kitchen, giggling over a pot of tea.

He loved his daughter and his wife more than he realized, but he hated it when they giggled together, it shut him out. Women's club. Also, it was worse, when he had someone with him. Worst of all when it was Charmian Daniels. Not that he disliked Charmian, she was an attractive woman, but she was a woman in a position of command, and that he did find difficult.

Deirdre and Fiona sitting comfortably at the table looked at his cross face and at Charmian whom they did not know. Fiona shook the pot. 'Empty.'

'Go and make some more then.' He pointed to the door to the pantry.

When it had closed behind her, his wife said, 'She might have difficulty in making tea out there, most of the tea-making equipment is in here. She knew you wanted her out of the way, you should have said so honestly.'

More perceptive than her husband, she had been worried about the girl for some time now. She had her own worries too, but that was a different matter.

Frank cut across what she was saying, 'Miss Daniels wants to ask if Fiona knows why an envelope addressed to her at this house was found in the jeans of the dead girl.'

'An envelope with Fiona's name on it. Had it been delivered?'

Quick of her, thought Charmian. But she was a lawyer, wasn't she? She'd gone pale, though.

'Yes.'

'Makes a difference.'

'I must ask her about it.' Charmian turned back to Frank Greenham. 'With you both here, of course.'

'Yes,' said Deirdre quickly, 'both of us.'

'And I will have to ask her to see if she can identify the dead girl . . . with you both there, naturally.'

'Wouldn't it do if you described the dead girl?' Frank Greenham asked. He had seen the girl's face and had no desire that Fiona should see the same.

'If she remembers to whom she gave the envelope or who might have had it, picked it up, something like that, and gives a good description of that person, it might do,' said Charmian, promising nothing. She knew that Fiona would have to be shown the body.

Fiona ame in with a tray. On it was a bottle and

four glasses. 'Couldn't find any tea stuff, anyway, I knew you'd prefer this.'

As a comment on the Greenham family life, it was interesting and instructive. The wine was a good claret too. All the same, Charmian refused it.

'Not for me, I have to drive off. You three are at home.

Fiona had opened the wine, she was at home with the bottle.

Frank Greenham and his wife took some wine, Fiona did not. She shook her head. 'Don't fancy it.'

'I bet,' said Deirdre.

'Some time soon,' said Frank, 'I'm going to be asking where you've been all this time. That is, if the Chief Superintendent doesn't ask first.'

Fiona turned her big, dark eyes on Charmian. 'I know you, Miss Daniels, You came to the school and gave us a talk on women in crime.'

'I hope it didn't inspire you towards a life of crime?'

'Wasn't meant to, was it? No, didn't make me want to be a police officer or a prison warder either. Thought I might write about it . . . You know, crime books.'

Sharp girl, they were well matched.

'That is an easier option,' said Charmian smoothly. She produced the envelope in a transparent plastic folder. 'This envelope is addressed to you.' It was a statement, not a question.

Fiona looked and nodded. She did not speak.

'Who is it from?'

'Mary James, a school friend, her parents broke up and her mother took her off to London.'

This was supported by the postmark. No reason to disbelieve her, of course.

'You took the letter out? Do you still have it?'

'It wasn't really a letter, not in the way you mean, it had a ticket for a concert I wanted to go to in it, and I went. Met Mary there.'

'When was this?' Judging by the postmark it could not have been long ago.

Fiona's eyes flicked to her father. 'Last night, that's where I was.'

'You slept there?' growled her father, not waiting for Charmian to speak.

'Well, sort of, it turned into a sort of party.'

'Sort of, sort of,' he was still growling. 'You're not old enough to be partying all night.'

Fiona blinked but said nothing.

Her stepmother raised a half cynical, half sympathetic eyebrow at her. If partying were all, it said.

Charmian broke into the family squabble.

'The envelope – did you throw it away?'

Fiona drew her lips together and frowned. 'No. Not sure what I did with it. Why?'

Not answering the question, Charmian thought. 'Try to remember.'

'Why does it matter? Is it important?' Was she vague or just pretending? 'I mean, you don't bother with envelopes, do you?'

'Just try.'

Frank Greenham stood up and banged the table. 'Come on, girl, give your mind to it. Try to remember what became of the envelope. Who could have found it? Where could it have got to?'

'But you know where it's got to,' said Fiona. She pointed at Charmian. 'She's got it.'

That's it, thought Charmian. This cheeky little miss is strong enough to see the dead girl.

'Fine. Let's get off. I am going to see if you can make an identification.' She turned to the parents. 'Of course, you will want to come. Yes? Right. How old is Fiona?'

She could be any age. Not as much make-up as the dead girl had worn, but a fair amount.

'Nearly fifteen,' Frank answered, his eyes on his daughter's face.

'Right.' Fiona's age would require the presence of a youth officer; she would set about organizing someone, she didn't know who was on call . . . Shirley Bendon was the likely one. Nice woman, practical and sensible, strong too, and goodness knows she needed to be all of that for the job she did. What was more, she was a quiet lady who did not interrupt when Charmian got on with her questioning. Charmian did not enjoy questioning children, although Fiona was one of the least childlike children she had met.

'Come on, then.'

'Where are we going?' demanded Fiona.

Charmian did not answer. She would find out.

As they walked to the car, Frank Greenham gripped Charmian's wrist very hard.

'You're hurting.'

He relaxed his grip. In a low voice, he said, 'I reckon this has something to do with Joan Dingham, and I am holding you responsible.'

Charmian did not answer, but she rubbed her wrist and looked away.

They went in two cars: Charmian took the girl and her stepmother, and Frank Greenham followed on his own, a dour figure somehow managing to make his presence felt even a car space behind.

Charmian understood his mood; she had kept the girl and his wife with her so that he could not influence what Fiona might say. She had chosen to have Deirdre Greenham with her so that no questions could be asked later about what she said to Fiona. Handling children was always tricky, there was no need to make the task harder.

Fiona and her stepmother sat in the back, silent. Charmian caught Fiona's gaze as she closed the doors and started the car. Some child, she thought, but with amusement. There was something endearing about this girl who had obviously been out on the town and didn't want to talk about it.

Charmian had checked for messages on her mobile phone and discovered that the body of the girl, the false Fiona Greenham, was now in the University Hospital. She knew the place. The university had been built recently and was situated in a new university park, out beyond Slough. The hospital, however, was old, a former workhouse, which dated it precisely as late Victorian rebuilding, which had been converted into a hospital several decades ago without being able to throw off the smell of its past. But University Hospital was an efficient, friendly establishment which the police found useful. Charmian was known there.

Dolly Barstow was waiting in the front hall, coat drawn close about her against a chill wind blowing through it, and taking irritable steps here and there at intervals.

She was pleased to see Charmian. 'They said you were coming. I came in with the body to do the official stuff. Someone had to and no one else seemed to be free.' She glanced across at Fiona and Deirdre who had just been joined by Frank Greenham. 'Who have you got there? Don't tell me, I can guess.'

'The girl is Fiona Greenham,' said Charmian.

Dolly raised an eyebrow. 'Looks like her dad. Is that the mother?'

'Step. The girl says she doesn't know where she lost the envelope, which I don't believe, by the way, and I have brought her in to see if she can identify the body.'

'Right. Tough medicine.'

'If I shake her up a bit, she might start remembering and talking.'

Dolly studied Fiona. 'I wouldn't have done at her age, I'd probably have clammed up more.'

'Let's hope she's not like you then.'

'We going in in force?'

'I don't know. I must take a parent with me, and I am waiting for the child protection worker.'

'I always think it's the social worker who needs protection, not the kid,' said Dolly. 'But if it's Shirley Bendon, then she's here anyway on some mercy mission and is just getting some coffee. She'll be radiant to see you, she's dead beat and hoping to get off home for some sleep.'

'You don't get regular sleep in this job.'

'I expect she's noticed.'

They could both see Shirley approaching with two

beakers of coffee. She handed one to Dolly and looked doubtfully at Charmian.

'I only got two.'

'That's all right, Shirley, I don't want any. Nice to see you.'

Shirley took a quick drink.

'It's work, I'm afraid.'

'Don't tell me, let me guess. It's connected with that kid over there.' She nodded at Fiona.

'You know her?'

'Not by name, but I know the face. She runs around with a crowd her dad would not like.'

'You know him?' Charmian was surprised.

'Lectures to me for the diploma I'm doing.'

'One big happy family, aren't we?' said Dolly.

'The girl is Fiona Greenham. She is coming to look at the dead girl, in the hope that she can identify her. Or help.'

She looked across at the trio who stood waiting. 'Well, off we go.'

They made quite a party going in to the mortuary: Fiona with her father, Charmian and Shirley and a young WPC who appeared from nowhere, not to mention Dr Chris Thomas, who was in charge of the mortuary, and his assistant.

Deirdre Greenham stayed outside with Dolly Barstow.

A drawer was pulled out from the wall, a white sheet over the form on it.

Charmian noticed with satisfaction that Fiona was pale as she was led up to look, and then was ashamed of herself for being pleased. She was only a girl, after all. But a resolute one. She nodded assent as the sheet was dragged back, stared quietly at the face, then nodded again.

'I do know her. I don't know her real name but I have met her.'

'No name?'

'There were loads of us at that party, jammed together, I was with a gang. That sort of party.'

'You gave her an envelope, though.'

Fiona took a deep breath. 'She was going to get me some stuff . . . Tablets.'

'Tablets? Like what?'

'Like E, I guess. Or sort of. Maybe. There was some money in there.'

She stopped again. Charmian could hear Dr Greenham muttering some angry words. That growl again. Well, he had cause, no doubt.

'So she knew your name, but you didn't know hers?' It made sense: the dead girl was an Ecstasy supplier.

'I did ask and she laughed. She said she was called Bibi and her mother was called Baby.'

Baby and Bibi, well, well, Charmian thought. Oh, God. There are complications here.

Another complication, although where it came into the web she was not sure, was Joan Dingham. You could say that Joan connected with Baby whom she certainly knows and now also with Dr Greenham.

Coincidence.

I am not a great believer in coincidences, thought Charmian. They happen, of course, but I don't like them so close to murder.

Across the road, she could see Chief Inspector

Webley and Inspector Round getting out of their respective cars. She decided to give them a friendly greeting, then leave them to it. She had set her own circuit in motion. Those sticky fingers, she had heard they spoke of had their uses.

On the drive home, Deirdre sat in the front next to her husband, and Fiona sat in the back.

'We'll need a solicitor, a good one.'

Fiona muttered something.

'Listen, I am an academic administrator,' said her father sharply. 'I know what the word drugs does to the police. You need legal help and that will cost.'

'There will be another cost too,' said Fiona, 'I'm pregnant and I don't want an abortion on the NHS. I want a private room in a good clinic. It'll cost.'

Chapter Three

'So who is going to tell Baby that her daughter is dead?' asked Dolly Barstow. She and Charmian were drinking coffee in Charmian's kitchen. Humphrey had just arrived back home after reporting that Birdie and Winifred (not to mention the so-called hermit) were anxious to know what news there was of the body that had been found not so far from the bottom of their garden. This had happened to them before.

'Tell them nothing,' said Charmian. 'Let's wait and see.'

'So I told them.' He poured himself some coffee. Under his own careful tuition, Charmian's taste in coffee had improved. This was good Java. 'They didn't believe that, of course.' He took a long drink. 'Neither did the hermit. Passionately interested he was, but not saying a word.'

'Who is that man?' demanded Charmian irritably.

'A liar, to begin with.'

'Oh?' said Dolly with interest.

'It wasn't chance that brought him to the shed in the witches' back garden. He knew where he was going.'

'I wondered about that,' said Charmian, 'and I thought Winifred did too.'

'He probably sussed the place out before he came to Windsor,' said Dolly.

'Wonder why he was there?' said Humphrey. Then he answered his own question. 'It's more comfortable than Pinckney Heath.'

'Something to do with the murder of his granddaughter,' said Charmian.

Dolly almost choked on her coffee. 'He'd never suspect the white witches? Not Birdie and Winifred. Although they have been mixed up in some funny business in the past. Look at the bodies in their bookshop . . . not their fault, goodness no, but there they were, close to it. They attract crimes, I think. Do you suppose it's being witches that does it?'

'I think it's what's known as being a focus for trouble, but I don't know what causes it, except I think those two have got it.' Charmian was half laughing. 'I suppose I'm a focus for trouble myself.'

'Not you,' said Humphrey. 'It's just your job, your *métier*, your profession, that's different.'

'Glad to hear it, I've sometimes wondered if I chose my profession, as you kindly call it, because of the way I was.'

'Someone has to tell Baby,' said Dolly. 'Take her to see the dead girl. It could all be a mistake.'

'That's a task for the uniformed branch,' said Charmian. 'Inspector Parker will sort that out! Joan Dingham arrived this morning so he can't send Emily Agent to speak to Baby.'

'You don't want to do it,' was Humphrey's comment. 'Can't say I blame you. Still . . .' He looked Charmian in the eye.

She sighed. 'Yes, I know, I'll be there . . . but uniformed must be there too.' She put the cup of coffee down. 'In fact, I've already set it up: I phoned through to Central, told them to send an officer tomorrow to take Baby to the hospital. I'll be there to meet them.'

'Supposing she says she hasn't got a daughter, never had a daughter and the girl is nothing to do with her?' said Dolly.

'And supposing she says Fiona is lying?'

Dolly nodded. 'Yes, that could be. But what an interesting lie.'

'What an unlikely lie,' said Charmian. 'Think about it. No, Fiona wasn't lying.'

'I don't get it,' said Dolly, who liked events to be crystal clear, even if it was nothing to do with her. 'What do you think?'

'We've a choice: either the girl was killed because she was Baby's daughter – father unknown, or at least unknown to me – or because she had that envelope in her pocket and the killer wanted to kill Fiona Greenham.'

'And supposing it was neither of those two motives?' said Humphrey. 'Sometimes I think you two women like to play intellectual games. What about Dr Harrie's granddaughter? Perhaps this death is one more in the chain.'

He whisked the empty cups away from them and into the dishwasher. 'Come on, off to bed. These problems will still be there tomorrow.' He looked at Dolly. 'Want to stay the night? The bed's made up, I'm a good little housekeeper.'

'No, thanks for the offer, but I'd better get back. Got to look after the cat.'

She took herself off, driving away into the night to

the small house in Merrywick where she lived at the moment: she never seemed to stay anywhere long. Too much money, was what Charmian said, she could pick and choose.

'Has she got a cat?' asked Humphrey.

'Don't know who or what she's got there,' said Charmian. 'There's usually a changeover and I'm usually a man or two behind.' She spoke absently, occupied with thoughts of the dead girl.

Identity, identity, identity.

Why had no family claimed her?

Dolly did have a cat, a thin striped creature who was asleep on her bed. 'You're all I have at the moment,' Dolly said half sadly, half with relief. 'It's a quiet life, but a comfortable one. I think I'm a spinster by nature, really. Not a virgin, but a spinster. An unmarried woman sitting in the sun spinning. Only I spin stories about death.'

There was no message on her answering machine and no e-mail. 'All right, you've gone for good,' she said, studying her computer. 'Just as well really, another policeman and a medical one as well, it would never have done. Still, James is a nice name, but there was never any chance I would marry you (not sure if that was what you wanted) or have your child. I shall remember you with pleasure, though maybe not with pride. And we will meet professionally.'

Dolly crawled into bed beside the cat who did not wake up. She closed her eyes and listened to the cat snoring but found sleep hard to come by. She was tired but could not sleep. All that coffee that Humphrey had poured out.

No, not the coffee, but Felicity Harrie and now this new victim, both murdered, almost certainly by the same person. Definitely murdered by the same person in her book. Same method of killing, manual strangulation, the body just left around to be found, cuts on the body, with vaginal assault. Felicity had been similarly attacked vaginally, although with lesser penetration. And both girls about the same age.

She could ask James more about the medical details, she could talk to him about the case, that was professional business.

'Dr Farmeloe,' she could say, 'what is your opinion of these deaths?'

Two murdered girls. What had they got in common to make them victims? Dig around, girl, she told herself, dig around.

No answer came.

Her sleep was restless, with the faces of the dead girls moving in and out of her dreams, but towards morning she slept heavily coming to with a jerk.

She went straight to the phone. 'Charmian? Listen, check if there is a link between the two girls, there must be one.'

Charmian and Humphrey slept better than Dolly but were up earlier. Charmian took the call from her. 'Yes, I thought of that,' she said calmly, 'and have already initiated a search. Rewley is working on it. I left a message on his answerphone.'

'They might have known each other.'

'Yes, I thought of that, too.'

Dolly felt abashed. 'Just an idea,' she apologized. 'Sorry to get you up.'

'We're up. Been up for ages.'

They had had to be because the boy who delivered their papers, they took a range from *The Times* to the *Mirror*, had come hammering on their front door when the sun was just rising. Behind the boy was a girl. She, too, was carrying a sack of papers.

'What's the trouble?' Charmian yawned. She reached out to take the papers. She didn't mind getting up early but it had to be from choice. To be summoned by a banging on the door was not what she enjoyed. Also, surely it was almost an hour earlier than usual?

Humphrey, of course, had not stirred.

Now she was more awake, she thought she knew the boy. 'We met yesterday.'

'Sort of met. I'm Peter Robb and this is Amy Fraser. We found the dead girl last night.'

'Evening, really,' said Amy, popping out from behind him. 'It wasn't so late.' She seemed anxious to establish the timing. She reached out to take Peter's hand.

'We wanted to tell you something,' Peter spoke quickly.

Amy broke in, 'We don't want to be a nuisance.' She seemed on the point of dragging Peter away. 'And we ought to get on with the delivery, people will be looking for their papers.' She gave them both a radiant, anxious smile.

Peter took his hand away. 'Don't, Amy. We agreed to do this. And we're early, it's why we are so early, we can catch up.'

Charmian could feel a chill wind blowing down the

street. 'Come inside,' she said to them. 'I don't know what this is about but I am not going to talk on the doorstep.'

She led the way into the kitchen which was warm and tidy. Any food left over from last night had been tidied away, and the Aga was burning brightly. All this was due to Humphrey who had reformed Charmian's bleak kitchen.

She put the kettle on in order to make some tea. She didn't care whether these two wanted any or not, she did, at least two cups of strong hot tea.

'Tell me now what this about.' She had her eye on the kettle. The teapot was to hand. She could see the girl eyeing the pot with interest. No doubt in her house the teabags were popped straight into the mug.

'It's a teapot,' she said.

'Oh, I know, we've got my granny's but mum never uses it. Well, she doesn't drink tea unless it's herbal and she says it would be a waste to infuse it.'

Well, I deserved that, thought Charmian. Infuse it, eh? She has a way with her, this girl.

Peter said quickly as if Amy might stop him, or prudence rein in his tongue, 'We came because we didn't tell all yesterday.'

'Go on. You found the body. But it wasn't by chance.'

He was surprised. 'Yes, how did you know?'

'Because I hear that sort of story often.' It was rare in her experience that a body was found quite by accident. The finder often had a purpose of some sort in being where the body was.

Peter licked his lips. 'We were supposed to be meeting her.'

'Oh, were you? Strange place to meet.' She waited.

'We met her at a party the night before . . .' he paused.

'And you liked her so much, you wanted to meet her again?'

'No, no nothing like that. We just thought we'd meet and talk.'

'Oh, come on,' said Charmian, pouring water into the pot, and then getting three cups and saucers out of the cupboard.

'She was getting us something. Tickets for a concert.'

Charmian did not believe this for a minute, there had been no tickets on the body. For that matter there had been no Ecstasy tablets, Valium, or any money. Just empty pockets.

'Right, let's leave that for the moment. Did you notice anyone else there?'

He shook his head, the girl shrugged and said no, she hadn't seen anything.

'So what did you do?'

Peter was the spokesman. 'We saw someone lying there. Didn't know it was her at first.'

'I could see she was dead,' said Amy. 'I am going to be a doctor, so I knew what to look for. Anyway, she had no pulse and her eyes were fixed. She was dead before we got there.'

Peter spoke up for them both. 'I phoned the police on Amy's mobile.'

Charmian looked at the future doctor. 'It's my mother's but she's in the Valley of the Kings.'

'So . . . you knew her name and where she lived?'

Peter shook his head.

Surprise, surprise, thought Charmian.

'We just met at the party, you see.'

'What did you call her then?'

'Didn't really call her anything.'

'So you don't know anything about her? Can you recall anything? Think, will you?'

'I think she said she was called Pippa and her father was a poet.'

'And her mother?'

'Oh . . . dead, I think . . . she'd passed on.'

Charmian poured out three cups of tea. 'Thank you for coming. Drink that.' She pushed a sheet of paper at them. 'Write your names and addresses there, please, so we can get in touch.'

The two looked at each other. 'Our parents – ' began Amy.

'Yes, they'll have to know. You'd better tell them first.'

Humphrey appeared on the stairs behind her as she watched the pair depart. Paper deliveries would be late today.

'What's up?'

She turned to look at him. Not many men can look distinguished and intelligent when unshaven and sleepy, but Humphrey managed it. His old grey dressing gown was ragged at the edges, his slippers were soft and battered, but they were worn with unconscious style, looking as if they had come from Jermyn Street or the Rue St Honoré some decades ago. Which, come to think of it they probably had.

She poured him some tea. 'Here you are, hot and strong.'

'Good, I can't abide weak tea,' he said with the

complacent air of one who had wed an obliging wife. He was in charge of the coffee while Charmian took care of the tea, but he had had to train her. At least she went to the best stores now. 'So what was all that about?'

'The couple of kids who found the body last night are also the pair who deliver our newspapers. I didn't know that.'

'Did they come to tell you?' Humphrey finished his cup of tea and poured another one. 'Want some more tea? I'll have to put some more water in.'

'No, thank you,' said Charmian, her voice abstracted.

Humphrey sipped his tea, the second one always tasted best of all, and studied her. 'So what did they come to say?'

'They not only recognized me, knew me, they also knew the dead girl.'

'What?'

'Yes, bit of a surprise that. I think they were going to buy some drugs from her, not that they admitted it. They made up some story about trying to get hold of concert tickets. They met her at a party. I daresay the girl Fiona was also hoping for some of the same. May have bought some in fact. We'll have to go into that.'

'Does this help you?'

'It helps me build up a picture of the dead girl. She told Fiona that her mother was called Baby and she was called Bibi . . . I drew a conclusion from that: I decided that she was Beryl Andrea Barker's child.'

Humphrey nodded. 'Seems reasonable.'

'Didn't it? I haven't spoken to Baby yet, although I have arranged a visit to the mortuary with her to see the dead girl. That's not off. She shall go, but later, I will tell Parker.' And she would be there herself to see Baby's face.

'You don't think the dead girl is her daughter?'

'I'm leaving it all open. She told Peter and Amy that her father was a poet, and her mother was dead, passed over, as she put it, and she was called Pippa. I think she must have been reading Browning, don't you?'

'Not many people read Browning these days,' said Humphrey thoughtfully.

'And she didn't look like a girl who read poetry.'

Humphrey pointed out that he had, and he was glad about it. He had not seen the girl, but he could tell Charmian that Birdie and Winifred were wondering if they could identify her. There was a girl who had come in looking for a post in their bookshop and they wondered if it might be her.

Charmian groaned. 'Let's keep them out of it for the moment. We can reel them in later. They have their hermit, he's enough to keep them occupied surely.'

'They're bored, I think,' said Humphrey. 'I detect a slight drawing away from white witchery.'

'Their life seems full enough to me, with their bookshop.'

'Just warning you.' He finished his tea and picked up the pile of newspapers. 'I fancy there is a distinct movement towards crime. Birdie and Winifred, Detectives Ltd.'

'I hope you are joking.'

'Half and half . . .' his voice was abstracted. The local newspaper had fallen out of the pile and the headlines had caught his attention.

ANOTHER MURDER VICTIM. DO YOU KNOW THIS GIRL?

Underneath was a drawing of a young girl. She had a neat-featured, pretty face, her hair falling, straight and plain, over her shoulders. Her face was heavily made up.

Charmian grabbed the paper. 'Let me look . . . It's not a bad likeness. Whoever drew this saw her, and I want to know how.'

'If you read on,' said Humphrey who was reading over her shoulder, 'you will see that the editor says he was sent the picture from an anonymous source. Arrived on his desk.'

DID THE KILLER SEND IT? asked another headline.

'Why hasn't he sent it to the police? I should have had it.'

Humphrey said nothing, he could think of several good reasons why the editor had kept it to himself, and the first and strongest was that the police would have retained it and used it as they thought fit rather than allowing him to print it.

'I am going to ring the editor and demand he send it round.'

Humphrey looked at the clock. 'Far too early, he won't be there. Might not be anyone there.'

'It's a newspaper office, damn it.'

'Not Fleet Street though. Or wherever the big nationals are now.' The local newspaper office was in Merrywick, housed in a quiet back street in a building that looked ancient outside and not much newer inside, although it was equipped with all the flashing screens and fax machines without which no office felt itself authentic. But Humphrey had called on the editor Percy Clubb once before about an article on the local theatre he was proposing to write and knew Percy to be a polite, gentle man, not in love with dazzle and push. He knew that what his readers wanted to hear about was the local deaths, births and marriages, together with some discreet gossip. Also wanted were careful reports of all local sports matches.

'I'm going to ring him. Someone will be there,' said Charmian.

The officer cleaner, thought Humphrey, or just the answerphone. Sometimes he thought that so many years as a high-ranking police officer, telling people to jump and watching them jump, had cut Charmian off from the world others lived in, the world in which people said no, or I might, or didn't even answer.

She did get an answer. A soft, young, female voice answered and acknowledged that yes, this was the *Merrywick Mercury*. Charmian could never shake free from the notion that this Mercury was a bisexual god who sometimes spoke with a gruff male voice, local accent, and sometimes with an educated, female alto. It was a different voice altogether today. That made three Mercurys. Marvellous theme for a really Attic comedy.

Charmian demanded to speak to the editor.

'The editor is not here yet, this is Ellen Dane, I am a reporter.'

A very junior reporter, Charmian thought, who would move on as soon as she got the chance. Percy was a good editor, careful and meticulous, no one could say he was zestful, or full of original ideas, or a man with his foot on the ladder, but coming from his stable you were well trained.

'Can I help you?'

Charmian speedily announced who she was and

what she wanted and heard a quick intake of breath and a moment of silence.

'I want the original drawing of the murdered girl that appears on your front page and I want to know where you got it.'

Ellen Dane said nervously that she couldn't do that, not without Mr Clubb's permission, and he wasn't . . .

'He isn't there,' said Charmian. 'I got that the first time. I shall send someone round.' She added deliberately, 'In fact, I might come myself. Let the editor know.'

Humphrey shook his head at her. 'Sadism.'

'Well, I'm not going to be pushed around. Not that Clubb can push anyone, but his reporter hasn't grasped that yet. She will. The last one did.'

She was dressed and was contemplating the breakfast which Humphrey had prepared, toast, scrambled eggs and coffee. He said he liked a good breakfast, which Charmian did not and probably could not cook, and he had added a curl or two of crisp bacon to his own plate, when the telephone rang. It was the editor of the *Mercury*.

'Clubb here, I am told you want me.'

'It's about the picture of the murder victim you have on your front page.'

'Oh yes. I thought it might help in establishing her identity.'

He talked like that, which was probably why he had never got to a big London daily. She had been in his office several times so that she could imagine it now: his desk neat but piled high with papers and folders; he himself dressed in jeans and a checked shirt, although he was too fat and too old for such clothes.

'I will send someone for it.'

'I can fax it to you.'

'I want the real thing. How did you get it?'

'It was hand delivered. We thought it was a joke or a phoney likeness but I sent Ellen round to the hospital to see if she could get a look at the dead girl.'

She obviously had done; she must be tougher than Charmian had thought. Not everyone fancies a late-night trip to the mortuary.

'We didn't plan to use it till the last minute or else, of course, we would have got in touch with the investigating team. Would have done today, anyway.'

'I'll get a message to Inspector Parker who is in charge of the investigation. He will send someone down.'

It was likely that Parker had handed over the case to another officer since his prime responsibility at the moment was Dingham. It would be some time before she earned the right to a first name again. That time might come, if she remained a good girl.

'I have offered to fax it to you, although I am not sure if it would fax well, the paper is thin.' Clubb was fussing.

'No, I want the original.'

Why was he so nervous? Charmian asked herself. She had once almost had him arrested for hanging on to a vital bit of evidence in a fraud case. He wouldn't risk that again.

Neither would she, for that matter, since her pressure tactics then had been the tiniest bit phoney, not to mention hard to carry through if she had had to do it. But sometimes a threat was enough as it had been then. He was not a brave man.

'You shall have it. I hope it wasn't wrong of me to

use it? I thought it might help. We didn't use the first picture. Thought about it but decided against it. It was more unpleasant, not just the face, you know, but the body as well.'

Charmian, who had been dressing and applying make-up while she spoke on the telephone, put down her lipstick. She had a bright red upper lip and a distinctly paler lower one.

'What are you talking about?'

'The Pinckney Heath victim. It was a drawing of her or at least the sender claimed it was. Didn't I make myself clear?'

'No, you did not.'

Clubb started to make a muttered apology.

'Hang on there,' said Charmian sharply. 'I am coming to collect both pictures.'

She sat thinking, lipstick in hand.

'What's up with your face?' asked her husband, interested. 'I like matching lips far better.'

Charmian finished her lips. 'I was thinking.'

'Somehow I guessed that. About the dead girl? Am I allowed to ask?' Charmian had been strict with herself when she married. Some information was confidential and restricted. Even her husband was not to be told.

But in this case, it was hard not to talk to him. She trusted his discretion.

'This is just for you to know.'

He put a finger on his lips. 'Not even to the cat.'

'The editor of the *Mercury* has a drawing of the girl found dead on Pinckney Heath.'

'Not your case,' said Humphrey.

'The style makes it probable it's by the same artist,

if you can call him an artist; the picture of the Windsor victim is rough enough work.'

'You're angry,' said Humphrey.

'Wouldn't have been involved if it hadn't been for the Greenham's daughter being named and if Dr Greenham had not been Joan Dingham's supervisor.'

'But that's not why you are angry?'

'You know me too well. No, I am angry at the way the editor sat on the letter saying a picture would be coming. Perhaps two pictures. Both vital. Pictures one and two as the sender fancied. The text was composed of words cut out of the local paper. He ought to have handed it over to the investigating team. The killer might have been traced and this second death avoided, if the killer of both girls is one and the same.'

'Wonder why he didn't hand it in? Not like Clubb. He belongs to my club in Egham. A decent chap.'

'I mean to find out.'

It'll be down to money and circulation figures, thought Humphrey, those are Clubb's twin worries. He was going to use the pictures somehow.

'She was a joker, that girl.' Charmian pulled a comb sharply through her hair, then stopped, it had looked better before she had touched it. 'Baby and Bibi, and then the poet dad and the mum that passed over.'

'You mean she deserved to die? Not like you to be vindictive.'

'No one deserves to die that way.'

She kissed his cheek, grabbed a coat and departed.

There was a lot of anger floating around in Charmian today, he thought.

Once in her car and driving towards her office on

the further side of Windsor, Charmian picked up her phone.

'Dolly, I want you to join me at the *Mercury* offices.'

Dolly was dressed, eating what passed for breakfast in her life, a banana and some roughage. 'Early for a press call.'

'I want to intimidate someone.'

'I think you can do that on your own.'

It was true. Charmian when angry, and even when not, could be formidable.

'It always helps with the press to have a witness.'

Does it? thought Dolly. So I'm a witness am I?

Because she drove faster and lived nearer to the *Mercury* offices in Merrywick, Dolly was there before Charmian and sitting in her car at the kerb waiting.

She watched Charmian arrive and get out of her car. Now, should I tell her that her lipstick is crooked? she wondered, and decided not. Definitely not.

Charmian saw her as she got out of her car, nodded at her, and together they moved towards the *Mercury* offices.

From her desk by the window, they were observed nervously by Ellen Dane (this was her pen name, not her real name), who had been told by Clubb to be his early warning system.

'She's a monster that woman Daniels when she gets going, and I want to know as soon as she arrives.'

Ellen knew Charmian by sight, she had seen her at a prize-giving which she had covered for the paper at which Charmian had spoken. She admired Charmian and, covering fashion for the *Mercury*, knew that the suit she was wearing was Armani. Wrong colour for her, though.

'Come on, girl, get on with that report.' The editor had his own way of showing his nerves.

'She's just arrived, Mr Clubb.' Ellen listened. 'That'll be the lift coming up now.'

It was an old building and the lift announced its arrival from floor to floor. A warning not without its uses.

'She's got another woman with her,' she announced; she could see through the glass.

'Who is it?' Clubb was standing up, studying himself in the mirror, smoothing his hair back and adjusting his spectacles.

'Another detective, I expect,' said Ellen. 'Nice haircut. Alfredo, at a guess.'

She was the product of a smart girls' school, and every so often her accent and her carefully casual, absent-minded but expensive style of dressing, irritated her boss.

'For God's sake, try to drop that debby accent and stop being so upper class.' He went back to his desk to sit down, the editor at work.

Ellen was hurt. 'It's just the way I am.' She was the daughter of a wealthy banker and a former stage beauty, now retired into private life, but Ellen wanted to be independent.

'Sorry.' Clubb took a deep breath. He fancied her, hard not to, she was vibrant with life and hope, but the existence of a wife with a wardrobe of matching shoes and handbags collected over twenty years held him back: he had learned to admit defeat.

The lift had arrived at their floor, the doors opened with a metallic sound, and the office doors opened. They were never locked during the day, this was a newspaper after all and should always be wide open to the world.

In spite of the secrecy maintained by the police and the prison authorities, Clubb was a competent journalist who had his contacts, especially in academic and literary circles, whom he kept well watered, so he had known before most that Joan Dingham was coming to study at the local university, he even knew which subjects she would be studying. He had been planning a special article on her which he had been working on alone. Charmian Daniels, never an easy lady to deal with, however, might have other ideas, so above all, he must not alienate her. It might still go ahead. Brilliant he might not be, but dogged and persevering he was. Dr Greenham he knew, at least by sight, but he must find a way of meeting Joan Dingham. She was said to be willing to meet the press and TV crowd. All this was talk among the media hacks but it seemed to be true.

He stood up as Charmian and Dolly came in.

'Do come in, sit down. It's Inspector Barstow, isn't it?' He managed a smile for Dolly and exerted himself to draw up chairs. 'Would you like some coffee? Ellen, make us some, could you?'

Ellen, glad to disappear, made for the door. But she knew her turn was coming. Yet after all, she told herself, I didn't do anything. But sometimes not doing was worse and this looked like being such an occasion.

'Can I have the drawings, please,' Charmian asked.

'Drawings.' He looked around. 'Now where are they?'

'I don't suppose you have lost them,' said Charmian bleakly.

'Oh, no, no.' He fumbled, pulling at papers and blotters. 'They're here somewhere.' He drew a folder from under a pile of books on his desk. You couldn't say he had hidden them but if he had not been obliged to produce the pictures, he would not have minded. '*Voilá*.' He held up a thin blue folder.

Ellen came in with the coffee just as he laid it in front of Charmian.

Charmian opened the folder and took out the drawings, placing one to the left, the other to the right. Then she sat looking at them.

'The one to my left is the Pinckney Heath girl, isn't it?' A question needing no answer. Clubb nodded. 'She was fairly badly cut up, I didn't know that. I've met her grandfather.'

'Haven't had that pleasure,' mumbled Clubb.

'If you could call it that. I hope he hasn't seen this drawing.' Not a question, but a statement.

Clubb poured out two cups of coffee which Ellen handed around. 'Not from us,' he said firmly.

'Us?'

'Ellen here.'

Charmian looked at Ellen. 'Yes, we will have to talk.'

Dolly moved across to look at the pictures. She drew her lips down. 'Obviously a killer who likes to cut up his victims.'

'So how did you get hold of these pictures?'

Clubb looked at Ellen. 'I found them,' she said.

'How did you find them?'

'Outside my door. On the mat. I have a basement flat in Waterloo Street.'

There was silence for a moment while Charmian stared into the girl's face.

'Not both together?' Charmian's voice was cold.

'No. One after the other.'

'That's a very strange thing. Didn't you think so yourself?'

'Yes,' said Ellen.

'Any idea how it happened?'

Ellen looked at her hands. 'I went to a party, one of those university parties. I was shouting my head off about how much I would give to get my hands on something about the Pinckney murder – I'd write it up, perhaps make it into a book, get a telly programme out of it. Next day, the first picture was on my doorstep.'

'And you did not hand it over to the police team?'

'Privilege of the press.' But Ellen's face was flushed. 'All right, it was wrong. And the second picture . . . well, we knew that one had to go to the police.'

'We?'

Clubb spoke up, 'I am more to blame than Ellen, I take responsibility. I wanted to use the pictures . . . The first one, I thought we could hang on to, see what happened, where the police investigation got to. It didn't seem to get anywhere, I think you must agree there.

'Not my case,' said Charmian tersely. In fact, she agreed but was not going to say so. She could even understand the entrance (in what she thought of as fancy dress) of Dr Harrie and his dog. There was something about the title of Dr in this case that she found oppressive: Dr Harrie, Dr Greenham . . . clever, well-educated, good-hearted men no doubt but they worried her.

The editor of the *Mercury* had known that she had nothing to do with the first murder case, even Daniels was not everywhere, and he would have preferred she had nothing to do with the second one, but she seemed to have walked into it.

He bowed his head, by way of acknowledging that he had been in the wrong without actually admitting it. Safer. You could never tell what trouble words could bring you. 'The second drawing . . . well, I knew then the police must have it.'

'But the newspaper had it first.'

'I was going to send it round.'

'I hope that is true.'

He felt like bowing his head again, because, in fact, it was not true. Finders are keepers in the newspaper world. But he had not taken legal advice (the *Mercury* could not afford it) so he was on uneven ground, might trip up.

'I will leave that for the moment, Mr Clubb.'

He did bow his head at that: he might be a friend of her husband, meet him in the club, take a drink with him, but Charmian was not showing friendliness. A lot was implied in that phrase 'for the moment' and none of it comforting.

Charmian turned to Ellen. 'I am going to ask you to write down the names of all the people at the party who might have been listening to you.'

'I might not remember,' said Ellen quickly.

'Oh, come on, you're a journalist. You've got a good memory. Names and descriptions, please. And, of course, who gave the party and where it was.'

'In the university,' said Ellen, feeling wretched. 'One of the big common rooms.'

Charmian did not give an inch. 'Good, so you've remembered that much. It's a start. And you had an invitation, someone asked you.'

'I just dropped in, you know how it is: you hear

about a party.' She shrugged. 'If you're in the mood, you go. Take a bottle and join in.'

'All-night party, was it?' Dolly spoke up.

'Might have been, I didn't stay that long.'

'Meet any people you knew?'

'Some.'

Dolly looked at Charmian, who said, 'Let's have a list – we'll put a star by them because they knew you and where you live.'

'Yes, can do,' said Ellen.

Clubb, who had been quiet but watchful, interrupted. 'Now is that all? We've got work to do.' Don't bully us, was what he was really saying. We are the press and have our own liberties and powers.

Charmian tucked the folder containing the drawings under her arm. At the door, she said to Ellen, 'Do you know a girl called Fiona Greenham?'

Clubb shuffled the papers on his desk.

'I don't know, don't recognize the name . . . Might know her if I saw a photograph.'

As Clubb got up to show them to the door, he upset his cup of coffee which he had not touched. Ellen leapt forward to help him.

Charmian and Dolly escaped while he was mopping up.

On the stairs, Dolly said, 'Did you believe all that?'

'She wasn't telling all the truth.'

'He was protecting her.'

'Or she was protecting him,' said Charmian.

'I've met her before.'

'I wondered about that.'

Dolly was surprised. 'Did you?'

'The way you looked at her. She didn't know you, though.'

'No,' Dolly was opening her car door. 'And I can't remember where I met her. But when I do, I'll let you know.'

'I expect it was at a party,' said Charmian, straight-faced.

Chapter Four

Charmian had a neat pile of two white and two blue folders on her desk which she was working through one by one, hardly raising her head. Her secretary was dealing with routine matters. Charmian had sent Dolly and Rewley out.

Dolly had taken the order calmly, and Rewley had pointed out that he was already at work trying to find links between the two dead girls and was in fact speaking from his mobile in a coffee shop they might have used. 'Not much else open when I started out,' he had said, sharply for him. 'I am trying to work out the approach.'

'I have one that might help,' and Charmian gave him the *Mercury* address.

Dolly was at the local university checking on who had given a large party the night before last, who had paid for the room and, if possible, who had gone to it. Her hopes were not high about the guest list. Her own university days were not so far away that she did not know about gate crashers. You didn't call them that any more – just extras.

Rewley was on his way to the *Mercury* offices to talk to Ellen Dane. Ellen would like Rewley, thought Charmian. She would find him interesting and attractive, perhaps even plan to write an article on him, and find out later that he was ruthless. Charmian herself had learnt to be wary of Rewley. But she respected his intelligence and was pushing for him to be promoted to Chief Inspector, as the CID link between the home force and the Met. The way things were going all the CID forces were going to be interlinked.

Dolly Barstow would stay because her social life in Windsor and the county pleased her. One day she would marry, and marry well because it would be for money and position, and then she'd be off. The only protection Charmian had against guilt feelings when she harboured such thoughts about Dolly, who was a friend, was that she sensed Dolly was eyeing her own job.

Ambition, ambition, she thought. Watch it, Dolly, I haven't gone yet.

Meanwhile, Charmian made use of the ambitions and energies of her two assistants. She worked them hard.

Charmian finished giving all the files a quick read through. The forensic report on the first murdered girl, Dr Harrie's granddaughter, made painful reading. She hoped he would never see it. She had been cut about, with a sharp pointed knife, possibly before she was dead.

The palms of both hands had been scored with a cross.

Charmian turned to the first forensic report (there would be another, more detailed report later) on the second victim, so far nameless. On the right hand of this girl a cross had also been scored. At this point, she heard Dolly return from her visit to the university.

'Any luck?'

'A name or two, nothing as formal as a guest list, but the girl who hired the room and said it was her birthday party is called Freda Mercer, she's a post-graduate and lives out in Slough, I have the address and I plan to go there. The party had caused a bit of trouble because of its size and the noise they made but Mercer saw the place was left tidied up and paid the fee for hiring it, so no one is too cross with her.'

'Did you ask the people who let the room to Freda about Fiona Greenham?'

'Yes, the name didn't register, nor did Ellen Dane's but I didn't expect it to, I mean the woman simply let out the room and took the money. Freda Mercer is, in fact, Dr Mercer by the way.'

Charmian groaned. 'Another one.'

'Yes, so I'll be off to see her. Anything from Rewley?'

'Not yet.'

'I expect Ellen Dane is fancying her chances with him, she looks like a girl who strikes out, but I could tell her she is wasting her time. Rewley keeps work and pleasure strictly separate.'

'Don't go yet. I want your opinion on something.' Charmian drew out the relevant pages of two reports on the victims, and watched Dolly's face as she read.

'Same killer,' she said, as she looked up. 'That was suspected, wasn't it? Certainly makes it clearer.'

'Yes,' Charmian nodded then pushed across one of the white folders. 'This comes from the Dingham cases. Take a look.'

Dolly gave her a questioning look as she took the file, and this time she read more slowly. There was more to take in with four cases. Some of the pages were yellowing after twenty years spent sitting in the folder.

Dolly read with care and she went back to re-read some passages. Then she sat back. 'Well, similar cuts on the hands of the victims. Might mean something to Dingham, although she never said what as far as I know.'

'But what does it mean now? To us.'

'Could just be copy-cat murders, it happens.'

'Yes,' agreed Charmian, taking the folders back. She was troubled. 'But I want to know why.'

Rewley came in at that moment. 'Got some names from the girl. She knew a few of the people at the party, and she knew the chap she took to it. I know him too for that matter: he's a police constable, graduate entry. I'll look him up. I've made a list of the names she gave me and I'll work on her for more. She knows some more. She's given us a carefully sanitized list of people who wouldn't care one way or another if we got their names.'

'Did she know Freda Mercer, the giver of the party?'

'Slightly, she says. Somewhat more than slightly, I think, but I'll find out.'

'Do that, but meanwhile, take a look at these.' She pushed the folders towards him. 'I've marked the places I want you to read.'

Dolly poured some coffee for all of them while Rewley read. He was a fast reader, flipping the pages over quickly.

'I see why you wanted me to read and compare. The cutting on the hands in these murders does resemble those in the Dingham killings. I didn't know about them, by the way. I was still at school and, although I read about them, I don't remember much of the detail. I don't even know if the fact about the cutting on the hands was in the papers.' He started to drink his coffee. 'You think it's a deliberate copy?'

'Could be. But why? And why now?'

'To celebrate Joan's release from prison?' he said lightly. 'Could be.'

'Some joke,' Dolly was not amused.

'Did I say it was a joke?'

Charmian finished her coffee, then stood up. 'I don't know the score, but I know what I am going to do next. I am going to see Baby.'

She debated silently which of them to take with her.

Baby lived above the shop and on this day of all days she wished she didn't. She could smell the day approaching with enormous speed like a train. She put her hand to her aching head – the result of her own party for her so-called friends: Joan Dingham and her acolytes, or disciples, if you could call them disciples. Disciples who could talk, laugh and drink champagne.

I'll never be a disciple. Baby told herself, although she did admit to feeling some of the others' strange attraction to Joan, and she had certainly had her share of the champagne. But to be fair, although Baby had provided the champagne and the room for the party, Lou Dingham had insisted on paying.

It might have been thought odd that the party to welcome Joan had not been held where Lou lived, but it was what Baby would have expected. The sisters always kept their own place what they called 'private', which meant only what suited them. This had led to difficulties for the police investigating them who had tried to get evidence that matched her up with the profile of the killer they had put together. The police had had to get all sorts of special warrants and orders: the Dingham home was definitely not one you dropped into.

'We feel safe with you, Baby,' Lou had said, on thanking her as they left. Joan hadn't said anything.

The hairdresser's salon was already open and working. This was because Baby encouraged clients working in the shops and offices around her to come in for an early-morning wash and blow dry, or a trim, and why not have a manicure while your hair dried? Start the day looking good was her slogan. She had it painted on a silver banner across her window and it was printed on all her business cards and invoices.

The early appointments were popular, but, of course, it meant that Baby herself, not by nature an early riser, had to get up too and come into the salon. You didn't get discipline in your staff if you didn't follow the rules yourself. That was a disadvantage, although one she bore bravely; the advantage was that she, too, could have a cut and a blow dry at the beginning of the working day and look good. Appearances mattered to Baby. And, of course, her own appearance – as an advertisement for the salon – was good for business.

She had male clients, too. Old and young, all colours, an ethnic mix.

This had not surprised her, it was not due to luck but to her own planning: she had taken great pains in putting together a staff of highly attractive as well as efficient hairdressers of both sexes, because her clients had a variety of sexual inclination. Baby was not a prude and was by nature open-minded on such matters. Her chief assistant, a man called Bobby, had a succession of lovers, beautiful boys some of them, most of whom came in to get their hair trimmed here. She kept her prices moderate (although not cheap) so that no one felt overcharged. Naturally, by the time a client had had a manicure or a facial massage, and some of the 'special' lotion for the scalp the bill was not low. But the atmosphere was elegant and so comforting – it was surprising how many people needed comforting, as Baby well knew – that no one complained.

Charmian was a client, but not one who seemed to need comforting nor did she offer comfort or bring in a lover although Baby would have been delighted if she had. For many reasons she liked to keep on the right side of Charmian, and to have had a handle in knowing a weakness, like a lover, would have been useful.

Baby had made a modest advance to Humphrey one day when he had collected Charmian, by way of getting in the back way (she tittered when she said that to herself, really, Baby!), but he had said he always got his hair cut at the club and thought he got a good short trim.

Baby asked Bobby if everything was going smoothly or if there were any problems. And when he said not, but he would need a little time off, just a teeny teeny half hour or so, at lunchtime, and did she feel all right, because she looked a little bit off, Baby nodded her head, muttered something and shut herself in the office.

'All that drink,' Bobby had murmured to himself as he combed out a client's hair. 'Smell it on the air the minute you come in the front door.' To the client, he said, 'Just a little spray, dear? Our pine one is very good, such a lovely smell.'

In her office. Baby checked the day's post, drank some coffee and swallowed a couple of aspirins.

Her party still hung over her emotionally as well as physically. It had been a happy enough occasion on the surface, welcoming Joan, moving among friends. But there had been undercurrents. Baby had rated these as just her imagination, but no, there was conversation going on underneath the surface, jokes that meant something, though not to her. She had felt uncomfortable without knowing exactly why. So she had drunk more than she should have, not alone in that either, hence the headache.

But it was only as the party was breaking up that she had caught a snatch of conversation that her champagne-happy brain had almost edited out, but which came back to her now in the cold light of morning.

Diana's name had come into it. Diana King, it was hard to believe anyone still hated her.

Baby finished her coffee, took another aspirin, as the first ones weren't working, and told herself she was not going to think about the party and Joan Dingham and what she had heard there.

She was not pleased when a telephone call from Charmian Daniels told her that she was on the way over to talk to her. She knew Charmian's ways well enough to know that it had come via her mobile and that she was probably almost here.

But why?

She put on some lipstick and smoothed her hair. When she looked out of the window, she saw Charmian had arrived. She had a man with her. She recognized Rewley, although being a respectable business woman now, their paths had not crossed. In the old days, she would not have minded if they had since Rewley possessed just the kind of tough good looks that she fancied. He was also just the right number of years younger than she was to turn her on.

But somehow Rewley and Charmian Daniels arriving just at this juncture did not seem like good luck. Not chance, either. Something lay behind it.

Baby had her own bravery, she took a deep breath and walked out to face them.

'Hello, nice to see you. Two shampoos and blow dries, is it?' She put her head on one side as she studied Rewley. 'I'll get Bobby to do you, Inspector, if you don't mind waiting till he's through with his present client . . . Inspector Rewley, isn't it?'

Rewley agreed politely, but said he didn't really want a haircut.

'Somehow I didn't think so,' said Baby with a sigh, feeling her headache come back with renewed force. 'So what is it you two want?'

Charmian suggested they go into her office. She could see that several of the clients were watching, and would be listening too.

'Can't you talk to me here? I'm not going to be arrested, am I? Joke,' added Baby hastily. 'No, no, come along into my office, it's bad for business to have the police here.' How was it, she asked herself, that although both Charmian and Rewley were well dressed and acting politely, you could tell they were police on business? 'You spoil the colour scheme,' she added half to herself, although that was not strictly true since Charmian wore a dark grey suit and Rewley wore a dark blue one and the colour scheme of the salon was chic and up to date navy blue and grey. No silly pastel. Pink was out.

Following their reluctant hostess into her office, Charmian noticed the aspirin bottle on the table. Baby saw the look.

'Headache. We had a party last night for Joan.'

'I didn't realize you knew her that well.'

'I don't. I did it for Lou – she asked me if I would set it up. I didn't realize that she meant it to be here, but somehow that was how it ended up. I'm weak, you know, that's how it is. I let people push me around.' She was pulling out chairs for them. 'Sit yourselves down. Lou paid up, of course. Lou always pays her debts, every penny. She wanted to add twenty pounds, but I wouldn't have it. Didn't want a tip.'

'Of course not.'

'A hundred now,' said Baby with a grin, 'that would have been different.' Suddenly she felt better. 'Well, what is it you want? You didn't come, fully armed . . .' she cast a flirtatious look at Rewley ' . . . just to wish me luck.'

'You must have heard about the body of a murdered girl found on rough ground.'

'Not too far away from here,' said Baby with feeling.

'The dead girl had hinted to another girl at a party that she was your daughter.'

'What?'

'Just a hint, a suggestion, but it sounded to me as if she meant you.'

'I haven't got a daughter.'

'No,' said Charmian, thinking that not everyone admits to what they haven't got. Or might have. She kept her tone modest, moderate and quiet.

Baby rightly and instantly interpreted this as

meaning: I don't have to accept that statement, I might believe it or I might not.

Charmian looked toward Rewley, then nodded. He produced a photograph.

'Will you look at this? It's a picture of her.'

'Oh, I don't know, I don't know. Why should I?'

'To see if you know her,' he said gently. He held the photograph up in front of her. 'It's a drawing of her.'

'When she was alive?'

'Yes.' He had to assume this.

Baby took a quick look, then turned away. 'No, don't know the face.'

'Are you sure?'

Baby just shook her head. She didn't speak.

'I need to establish who the dead girl is.'

'Surely that's easy enough.'

'Not as easy as it might be.'

'You can have whole police teams working on it . . . Scientists and doctors, I read the papers, watch TV, I know what you can do.'

'There has to be somewhere to start. You may be it. Why did she imply she was your daughter?'

Baby just shook her head again. She didn't know anything and wasn't going to know anything. That was her classic, safe stand.

And who can blame her? Rewley thought.

Charmian took a deep breath: now comes the bad bit. 'I want to suggest that Inspector Rewley and I take you to see the dead girl . . . You might know her then.'

'You mean look at her? Dead, frozen . . . They put them into some kind of freezer, don't they?' Baby's tone was horrified. 'You can't ask that of me.'

'I'll be with you – we will both be with you.'

'And she can't spring out and grab me. You don't have to tell me, I know that. You think I've never seen a dead person, well, I have. When Di first went missing and we all thought that someone had got to her and killed her, I went to identify more than one dead body. It was never her. I ought to have known her better, wherever Di turns up dead it won't be in someone's bottom drawer.'

Baby felt better now she had got all that out and thought she might be up to going to see this dead girl after all. One dead person is not that much different from any other, she told herself. Some of the ones she had viewed had not died at all prettily, not at all.

'All right, I'll do it. But if I faint and break a leg, then I'll sue you for damages.'

That was the authentic Baby, thought Charmian. The one you didn't get to see very often but always knew was there.

'We'll see you don't fall. Rewley will hold you up.'

Baby slung her bag over her shoulder. 'I don't have to walk there, do I?'

'Rewley is driving us.'

'You're a good driver, are you, Inspector?'

'Of course.'

Baby smiled at him. 'Right, I'll sit in the front next to you then. I shall feel safe there. Protected.'

'And who's going to protect me?' murmured Rewley.

Baby's smile sweetened. She could keep this game up for a long while yet. Or, at any rate, as far as the hospital.

*

She was quiet as they walked into the hospital. After a few paces, she stopped. 'Why am I doing this? I don't have to do it.'

'You are doing it,' said Charmian gently, 'to help find the killer of a young girl.'

Baby looked her in the eyes. 'I notice you don't say: an innocent young girl.'

'I don't know how innocent she was, but she was not much more than fourteen so she hadn't had much time to be very sinful.'

'You think?' said Baby. 'I've met some!'

'Let's give her the benefit of the doubt.'

Charmian was easing Baby towards the entrance to the mortuary where a member of the uniformed branch, alerted by Charmian, stood awaiting them. There was just one pair of big double doors at the end of a long corridor.

Sergeant Derby acknowledged Charmian, Rewley and Baby. He knew Beryl Andrea Barker, she had a reputation. He did not follow them in; he had seen the kid's face once and that was enough. He did not know her.

'Soon in, soon over,' Charmian said to Baby.

Rewley went in behind them, the white-coated attendant slid open the drawer, then drew the covering from the face.

Baby closed her eyes. Charmian patted her arm. 'Come on.' Thus encouraged. Baby opened her eyes and looked. A longer look than might have been expected, then she shook her head and backed away.

She put her head down and walked fast, almost galloping down the corridor.

All the time, that snatch of conversation overheard

last night at the party which seemed in no way connected with what she had just seen slid in and out of her mind. It had been the one name which she had never thought to hear. Diana.

She concentrated on the dead face she had just seen, hoping to exorcise Diana.

When they were in the car, Charmian said, 'So it's no, is it? You don't know her, never saw her before?'

'Drive me back,' muttered Baby, her voice thick. 'Drive me home. I want to say something.'

When they got to the salon, she led them, through her own private entrance, straight to her office.

'Show me those drawings again.'

Rewley produced them, holding them out for her inspection. She stared at them, taking three deep breaths.

'I wasn't quite straight with you,' she said, looking up. 'I do know the faces. Both of them. Both girls came in here to have their hair done. Dyed red. They liked red.'

'Names, please,' said Charmian. They had an identity for the dead girl at last. After a name, surely an address and a family would be found?

'I must look at the appointments book,' muttered Baby. 'It's in the salon.'

The salon was emptying: it was a quiet day. Bobby had gone but Rachel and Dawn were still working. Rachel was combing out a client's hair, preparatory to cutting it, while Dawn was preparing the tint for a lady with greying hair who wanted to stay blonde. Several juniors hovered around holding brushes and lotions.

Baby turned over the pages of the appointment book looking at the names. 'Here she is: Wilhelmina Winkle.

Don't suppose it's her real name for a minute. She was a jokey character. It was a joke about being my daughter. She always paid cash, had it too, so no credit cards or cheques. She wasn't a cheque person.' The words were galloping out of Baby as she was turning back the pages. 'Here's the other one, but you know her name.'

'Did she use the name Harrie?'

'Yes. She was a different character from Willy Winkle.'

What's the connection, Charmian was asking herself, when Baby answered the unspoken question. 'They were friends, at the same school. I heard them talking.'

'Which school? Did they say?'

'Not so much a school as a college, sixth form college. That was it. They talked about computer studies. It'd be that place Priorsgate.'

And I bet the Greenham girl goes there, too, thought Charmian, so she can answer some questions. Gradually an identity, a background, although not yet a name and a family, was being built up for the dead girl.

Something else came into her mind: didn't Joan Dingham's son teach in Priorsgate College? He might have taught those girls. This was a thought to dwell on.

Rewley had one pertinent question to ask. 'Did you do their hair yourself?'

Baby answered at once, her face far from childish at that moment. 'Yes, I am the tinting expert.'

'So you knew the girls better than most.'

'I didn't know them at all really. They hardly spoke to me.'

Rewley showed his surprise. 'Did they come in together then?'

'Not always, but often. Sometimes one would come

to have her hair done and the other would talk and watch.'

'Strange kids,' he said to Charmian, as they left.

'Yes, and it's possible they were both taught by Pip Dingham. Check on that, will you?'

Left behind. Baby checked the bookings for tomorrow, and prepared to go up to her own apartment.

One of the junior assistants caught up with her to say that a lady had called to see her.

'Did she did leave a name?'

'No, but she said she'd be back.'

This girl is a moron, Baby thought, pretty but vacant. She ought to have got the name.

'I said you would be around.'

Baby nodded. 'I'll listen for the bell.'

She went upstairs and deliberately forgot all about it. She had had enough of the female sex these last thirty-six hours. She washed the thoughts away from her in a hot shower, during which she also washed her hair. Not all her hair, which was pretty, was her own, she had a small hairpiece which she washed and dried too. One of the good things about being a hairdresser was that you knew how to look after your hair.

Once all this was accomplished, she felt better. Cleaner and happier. After all, these terrible deaths were nothing to do with her. So she knew the victims? So what?

I've been a victim myself, she thought, more than once, and no one cried for me. And I didn't cry for myself, either. I like this Daniels woman, but she's a toughie.

In spite of her efforts to forget it, the whole conversation she had overheard last night came back to her. She knew the voices although she had been careful not to look at the speakers. It was loud and clear in her mind, but in fact it had been a whisper from behind the curtains. 'I didn't like her, and if there was a murder and I heard she was around, I'd think: she did it.'

'Is she that bad?'

'Manipulative. Wicked.'

'I've never heard you talk like this.'

'I hated Diana.'

In Baby's life, there had only been one Diana.

I knew the voices, she told herself, I believe I know who was speaking, but I can't be sure.

There weren't so many people at the party that I can't make a good guess. Lou was there, looking brassily attractive, as ever. Very like Joan in looks, but thinner and younger. She knew from her own experience that prison was both ageing and fattening. The food, she thought, and the lack of proper exercise.

Pip, Joan's son, had been there. A nice young man, polite and friendly. He didn't drink much. He hardly knew his mother – he'd only been a little boy when she'd gone inside. Creepy for him really to think of his mother as a murderer. Did he wonder sometimes why she hadn't killed him? But Joan was said to have changed, her actions had been explained as being due to mental illness, the result of the sudden death of her husband, from which she had now recovered. She certainly seemed intent on getting some education.

If there was anything in heredity, then Pip could be the local killer. But they said upbringing counted for more, and Lou had brought Pip up during his mother's enforced absence. She could hear Joan's voice at that party – she'd picked up a weird accent in prison, a touch of Birmingham mixed with a touch of Scots – 'Thank you for being such a good mother to my Pip. He's a good boy.'

Yes. Baby said to herself, and a good boy who has been the teacher of two murdered girls. Coincidence?

When you thought of girls that age being murdered, you also thought of sex and drugs, at least, I do, Baby thought, and I bet Charmian Daniels does. It's the sort of thing she'd be on to, and that Rewley.

Someone should tell Charmian about Pip and the two girls, but I don't think it's going to be me. Joan would kill me. Let Charmian find out for herself.

Baby wasn't hungry but she knew she must eat or tomorrow would bring not a simple headache but a full blown migraine. She got bread, cheese and butter out of the refrigerator and put some sandwiches together which she carried into her sitting room.

She was just about to open her mouth to start eating when she remembered the salon was not locked up. The doors would be closed and the blinds drawn, but the door would not be locked because that was a duty she reserved for herself. Groaning with self-pity, she went downstairs.

She locked the front door before going to lock the inner door of the salon. She had cleared the day's takings earlier.

Then she remembered the woman who was going to call.

There she was, sitting in one of the big chairs meant for decoration and not for sitting in.

'Oh my God, I forgot.' She could see the back of the woman's head.

Apologizing, she walked towards her. As she did so, the woman's head fell forward.

Baby stepped forward quickly. 'Here, are you all right?' There was a steady drip of blood on the floor. Baby began to shake. 'I don't know you, say I don't know you.'

But the woman was past speaking. It was Diana, and her throat had been cut.

Chapter Five

'God, you gave me a turn,' said Baby from the kitchen where she was making a sandwich and pouring out coffee. Her hands were still shaking.

'Just a joke.'

'A joke?' She came in with the sandwich and coffee to where Diana sat, with the flesh-coloured scarf with its very convincing looking wound. 'Is that what you call it?'

'A bloody awful joke,' volunteered Diana.

And then they both laughed.

'Why and how did you get such a thing?'

'Bought it in a shop off First Avenue in New York. They do such things very well over there. I got it for my nephew, little Freddy, but when I got home I found out he was six feet tall and studying computer science and logic at a local college here . . . Priory – something.'

'I know the place. Heard of it.' Baby watched Diana bite into a sandwich, and thought how thin she looked. Then she got back to her grievance.

'But why me?'

'I thought it would make you laugh,' complained Diana. 'It would have done once.'

'I've changed.' And so have you. Baby thought to herself. I used to think you were a beauty and so you were, Diana. But look at you now. She studied Diana's face: eyes rimmed heavily with deep black eyeliner, the lashes loaded with mascara and grey shadow on her eyelids. Her cheeks were red, too red.

Then she thought, but perhaps you'd look worse without it. A sobering thought.

Hair wasn't bad, it was probably a hairpiece.

She took a quick look at herself in the mirror on the wall. I've kept myself in better shape, she decided.

'And guess who is teaching Freddy?' Diana bit into the sandwich. 'Pip, Phillip, son of Joan Dingham. He's a teacher there, lecturer. I guess they call them all lecturers these days. I saw him, tall, well dressed, nice-looking, he didn't know me, of course, and I didn't introduce myself. Didn't say: I am an old friend of your mother's, we knew each other in the nick, and knew each other long before that, too. Didn't seem wise to say all that. I don't know if Joan wants to know me any more. I've been in touch, by post. Not much response. Didn't ask me to her coming out party. Yes. I know you had one.'

And that wasn't a total surprise, Baby decided. I know you better than you might think, you always did good intelligence work.

'What was that red stuff that I had to wipe up?' she asked.

'Some pretend blood, theatrical stuff. Guaranteed not to stain.'

'It had better not.' Although she had noticed it seemed to disappear as she mopped at it, she intended to check later. 'But don't give me another surprise like that one, will you?'

'Sorry.'

'I might not laugh next time.'

'You didn't laugh too much this time.' Diana took a swig of coffee into which she had poured some whisky. Without asking permission her hostess observed.

'I remember the time when we were both at school and you told me someone had set fire to my cat . . . I ran home, fast as I could, and Tibs was asleep in the sun. I was six and you were seven and splitting your sides with laughter. So no one knows better than me what your sense of humour is like.'

Diana nodded her acceptance. 'I'm a louse.'

'But when my cat really did die, run over, left in the gutter, you were the one who helped me bury it.'

'I didn't mind doing that.'

Somehow she could believe that burial was acceptable to Diana, it wasn't a joke, you didn't laugh, but it didn't worry you either. It was there for everyone, you had to accept it. Yes, even as a child there had been some strange sides to Diana's character.

'You're very thin,' Baby said, studying her old friend. If that was indeed their relationship.

Diana looked down at herself. 'True, so I am.'

'What were you doing in New York?' Baby asked.

'Working, of course. Running a bar.'

'I'd have thought you needed American citizenship to do that.' And no jail record. How did Diana do it? Lies, no doubt.

'Ha, ha,' said Diana. 'Is that your idea of a joke? Well, as it happens an English accent goes down well there.'

Oh, so that's what's happened to your voice, not Birmingham at all. How unkind of me to blame Birmingham.

'I liked working behind a bar,' went on Diana, 'nice people, and it paid well. I was out of prison on remission. But I had no money, alas.'

'So why have you come back?'

Diana allowed herself a pause before speaking. 'I'm dying.'

'Oh but . . .' began Baby.

'Yes, I know I died once, looked death in the face and it went away again, but it came back and this time it's here to stay.' She had had a brush with cancer once, as Baby knew, but now it had obviously returned.

For a minute, neither of them spoke, then Diana said, 'You've gone quite white. I can't join you, my colour is brushed on and fixed.'

'It was a shock. I'm sorry. I thought you looked ill, yes, and yes, I noticed the red on your cheeks, overdone I thought. Now I understand why.'

'Saw you looking. Nearly told you then.'

'Are you sure that it's as bad as all that? Nothing to be done?'

'Nothing more,' said Diana coolly. 'It's what they call pain control now.' She looked a her watch. 'Nearly time for my next dose.' Baby drew in her breath in a gasp, attracting Diana's attention. 'You all right yourself? You don't look it.'

'It was the party last night . . . Bee and Lou and all the Dingham lot. Celebrating, I suppose you could call it, although no one spoke to me much. Didn't say thank you as far as I remember, except for Lou. They don't like you, Di, I don't know if that worries you.'

Diana shrugged. 'Not a lot, not any longer. Is that why you look the way you do, kind of deathly, because of a hangover?'

'No.' Baby looked down at her feet. 'There's been a lot of talk about death for me today. I had to go and see if I could identify a dead girl.'

'And did you?'

'Yes. She'd been murdered. One of two girls . . . Both killed.'

'They shouldn't have let Joanie out,' said Diana.

'She didn't do it. She was still inside.'

'Sure? There was a chap in the States who used his time out of prison to visit his sick mother to put away a victim or two. I think he did seven like that.'

'I'll tell Charmian Daniels,' said Baby when she could speak. 'Her case, it is. She took me to the hospital.'

'We might have met then, I had to pop in this morning for a quickie appointment. The dead and the dying, poor old you. So, Daniels is still around, is she?'

'More important than ever.'

'She would be. I remember her; in a way, I liked her.'

'It's better to be on her good side,' said Baby dolefully. 'One thing I haven't told you is that both the girls went to the college where Pip Dingham teaches, in fact he taught them.'

Diana frowned as she finished her coffee. 'If I was your friend Charmian I would give Pip a good look over.'

'You can't inherit a taste for murder or catch it like a disease, can you?'

'You don't think so?' Diana laughed. 'Stick around, Baby.'

Her hostess sighed. 'Talking of staying, where are you staying?'

'Here, if you'll have me.'

'All right. For tonight anyway.' She knew it would be longer than a night: she had noticed the big black bag by the door.

They had a drink to celebrate the renewal of their friendship, even if it looked like being a short one, as Diana pointed out.

'Let's have one last little caper . . . Rob a bank or something,'

'There's a jewellery shop in Upper Line Street I've had my eye on.' Baby joined in her mood, more to adjust to the thought of Diana dying, again. 'Some lovely pearls there.'

'You have the pearls and I'll have the diamonds.'

'We ought to pass on most of the stuff,' said Baby severely. 'Can't wear it. Or not where it would be recognized. One row of pearls, yes, maybe.'

'Right. We'll share the profits, you can have most of it because I won't be around to spend it.'

'OK.' Now she knew for sure that Diana was ill: she never shared anything.

After she had seen Diana to bed. Baby went down to tidy up the salon.

Yes, Diana had been right, the fake blood had left no stain. Magic – a bit like Diana's life, thought Baby, and mine too, off we'll go and not a sign left.

She patted the china hand as she went past it and wondered once again where the hell the other one was. She had bought the pair in Paris in one of those once smart little shops in the Rue St Honoré, which had been blighted by tourists wanting to buy cheap mementoes with Paris written all over them. She thought her china hands had come from a jewellers or a glove shop, once chic, now passed away. But she liked them, and resented that the right hand had gone.

Why pinch a china hand?

Dolly Barstow was out working the university campus to see what she could pick up. So far not much.

Rewley was doing the newspaper and hospital circuit, likewise to pick up what he could. In cases like this you trawled. No other word for it.

Inspector Parker rang to say Joan and her sister were having an evening at home. Tomorrow they had invited a few people round to Lou's flat, Emily would be there and Parker had suggested asking Charmian.

'Emily Agent is with them. Joan seems to have taken to her.'

'That's good, makes things easier,' said Charmian.

'Emily's that sort, gets on with everyone. She's tough but doesn't let it show and I guess Joan realizes that having a bit of protection down here till she knows her way around is no bad thing. And Emily's a graduate of the university Joan's attending this month. She's seeing Greenham today, wants to get it over with, and Emily will go with her.'

'I hope he's calmed down.'

'A bit, he may be on the telephone to you but I've tried to sidetrack him to me or Emily.'

Charmian knew that Emily Agent was tough but canny, it was one of the reasons she had been selected for the job. Word had been passed down from Charmian's immediate superior: 'She's no wimp. I've seen Emily shin up a wall, then hop down the other side, and go running through broken glass to get her man.'

'Thanks.'

'Just warning you. He may get through, they're dogged these academics. Oh, and one more thing, Joan is going to the hairdressers tomorrow and guess who she has an appointment with? Baby Barker.' He was laughing, he knew of Baby's past and her record.

Did he know about the girls patronizing Baby's salon? Perhaps not. So Charmian told him and heard him draw his breath.

'Not sure if I like that, ma'am.'

Charmian, left alone in her office, was catching up with routine matters that the time spent on the two murder victims had left undone. She found routine work restful, and in a funny kind of way, it cleared her mind.

Presently she moved away from her desk to look out of the window at the views of Windsor. In the distance she could see the flag flying over the castle. Not the royal standard but the Union Jack, so the Queen was not in residence.

I need a blackboard so that I can chalk up all my problems and then stand back and look at them. She had the computer screen, so she could use that instead. It was the modern blackboard, after all.

What have I got? What I've got is an inquiry into two dead girls, murdered in the same way. And why have I got them? Because I am in charge of the welfare of Joan Dingham. The connection? Each girl has a cut on her hand which resembles a cut found on all of Dingham's victims. So is it anything to do with Dingham? Well, she was in prison, so unless she went missing and no one noticed, or she turned into an invisible woman with a knife, she didn't commit the murders.

Or did she?

Let's put that aside for the moment. I now know that both girls got their hair washed and cut, and sometime tinted, at Beryl Andrea Barker's hairdressing establishment where I go myself. And I know that because the girl claimed to be her daughter which Miss Barker denied.

Could it be true? Establishing the girl's identity would really help. And as a result of pressure on Miss Barker not only had she admited to knowing both girls but she had told us both girls attended the same school.

I have names. The Harrie girl. She consulted her list, Felicity Harrie, yes, that's her name. But the other one: Wilhelmina Winkle? She had a taste for making jokes that girl. A reader though, read Browning or so she had guessed. At their school they were probably both taught by Pip who is the son of Joan Dingham.

A kind of a circle.

She began to walk around the room, reminding herself that crime was only a small percentage of police work, and murder a small percentage of that number. She repeated it like a mantra as if saying it often enough would solve the case.

She went into the outer office which was empty, her secretary having left for home. There was a fair turnover of secretarial help in SRADIC. The work Charmian demanded was hard and intensive, alternating with periods when not much was going on. Like a war, she thought, which in its way it was. She switched off the computer screen which the girl had left on, then made herself some coffee.

She knew that the uniformed men were out doing the routine questioning of possible witnesses, that the grass and soil where the body had rested would be gone over, blade of grass by blade of grass, that forensic scientists would be examining the clothes of the victim, and that the dead body and the site where she had lain had been carefully photographed. Chief Inspector Webley and Inspector Ron Round were engaged in all this, SRADIC reported to the CID and the CID reported back, both parties being scrupulous with information without being overgenerous.

But all these things had been done for Felicity Harrie, except that Charmian had taken no active interest, and no good had come of them.

Dolly Barstow rang back at this point to say she had nothing new to report. But she would like to come in to talk, if she could.

Of course, she could. 'Be glad to see you,' Charmian said. Dolly's bracing cheerfulness was always welcome.

Although now she thought about it, Dolly had not been quite so cheerful lately. But it was no good trying to pick up your own good cheer from someone else: you had to brew it up inside yourself.

There was a knock on the door and Rewley came in. He looked exhausted but pleased with himself.

'We have the identity of the dead girl.'

'Splendid.' She got up, went to her private supply of whisky, and poured a measure for Rewley: he deserved it. 'I spoke to Ron Round on the telephone just now and he said that they were plastering the whole area with photographs of the dead girl hoping for a result,' she said.

He swallowed a mouthful. 'Touched up, I hope, I remember what she looked like when found.' He added, 'I got it from going through the school photographs for the last three years.'

'Round told me he was going to the school with the photograph.'

'I got there first.' He drank some more whisky. 'I'd have got there first anyway.'

Rewley never lacked in self-confidence and, on the whole, this was well justified, Charmian considered.

'Come on now, what did you do?'

He finished his whisky. 'I took an artist with me . . . Bone structure, relation of eyes to ears and cheeks and hair line . . . All tell-tale signs.'

'And what sex is this artist?' she longed to ask. Rewley's relationships were something she had long pondered. He kept his own secrets. Not her business, she didn't ask questions, although some would, but she would like to know. It was one point on which Dolly Barstow left you in no doubt. She had once revealed to Charmian, when somewhat more than drunk, that what she loved about her job was that there was so much sex around. The next day, remembering something of what she had said, she had tried to claw back the comment.

Charmian had read somewhere that in the police, if you've got any rank you needed to be whiter than white, but this did not seem to impede Dolly. It wasn't true, anyway.

'Yes, I got permission from the principal to take Lesley round.'

A neutral name. She suspected Rewley of knowing exactly what game he was playing.

'We got a copy of the large group photograph which the school has taken at the beginning of every year. Lesley went over each person with a magnifying glass. Took her time, she's very careful.' He looked at Charmian with a straight face. 'She picked out two possibles and one less likely.

He had the names:

Ursula Madden
Helen Mary Grey
Frances Jessimond.

'So which was it? Don't tell me you are going to say none of them?'

'You've read my mind – hard on Lesley, wasn't it? All three girls were there, and not dead and buried. But we got something because in the last group we went round, a girl came up and said she thought she knew who the dead girl was, someone called Marilyn Oliver, who did not belong in Priorsgate College but used to sneak in and use their swimming pool.'

'Is that all?'

'No, the girl, who was about four feet tall and the same square, said that she didn't think that was Marilyn's real name.'

Here Charmian gave a groan.

'Because she was a great liar,' said Rewley

'Don't tell me.'

Rewley held up a hand, he was enjoying every minute. 'My informant, called Jenny Brand, who would make a great gossip column writer, or even a TV chat show hostess if she grew a few inches and lost a bit of weight, because she is pretty enough, followed Marilyn one day and saw her going into the Lucy Pierce School of Acting in Flood Street. Jenny thinks Marilyn was her acting name.'

'I don't think I know the Lucy Pierce School.'

'Been in Flood Street some time, ma'am, but I don't think it would come your way. More a singing and dancing academy, not for preparing a student for the big thespian world.'

'You went there?'

'Of course, and I took Lesley who knows the owner, a former actor called Edward Warwick. Lesley described the girl and did a little sketch. And yes, they did know Marilyn, hadn't seen her for days, didn't wonder where she was because she was casual in her attendance. Not a bad student, but she was never going to get an Oscar or the lead at the National . . . Oh, and her name wasn't Marilyn. That was her professional name.'

'So what was it?'

'Phyllis Jones. And she paid her modest tuition fees herself. Delivered papers, perhaps sold other things. There was a slight hint that she was open minded about drugs and sex and might sell either. That's all they knew. The school is a fairly casual outfit but Lesley said the dance teaching was good. Well, goodish, she said.'

'But you got Phyllis Jones' address?'

'I got what they had – 2 Barton Street, Merrywick. I drove out there.'

He thought back to his visit. It was a small bungalow in the part of Merrywick nearest to Slough, the least expensive part. The curtains had been drawn and the house seemed empty.

He rang the bell but was not surprised to get no answer. As he stood waiting, just in case, a woman appeared next door.

'I was hoping to find Mr and Mrs Jones.' And to tell them their daughter was dead and why were they not worried?

'They're not there.'

'No,' he had grasped that much.

'And they're not called Jones, if you are wanting Jones, then you've got the wrong house. Siddons . . . That's the name.' She added, 'That's what they called themselves but it was a stage name, Mrs Siddons told me so, couldn't use their own name, not euphonic enough . . . I think that was the word.'

'Ah.' Somehow he believed that. Not that Siddons was their real name, which probably was Jones, or Smith, or Willis, or Brown, but that it was their professional name. At last he felt he was getting nearer to finding out where the girl had lived. Names didn't matter here, you chose what you wanted.

'Away in South Africa. On tour. Theatricals.'

'Oh.' What else could he say? It fitted in with what he knew of the girl's life.

'The girl was supposed to be there, looking after the cat. She hasn't been near the place, I've got the cat now.' The woman looked down to where a lean and sinewy tabby was winding itself about her legs.

I reckon you've got it for life, lady, Rewley said to himself. 'Can I have your name?'

'Mrs Armstrong, and I live next door.' She nodded. 'But you know that.' She had shrewd eyes in a lined face under greying hair. 'Four Barton Street. I'm on the phone.'

'Thank you.'

'They're nice people, kind,' she said, looking at him. 'I hope there's no trouble. I liked the girl you know, Elizabeth, even if she was a bit wild. You're a policeman, aren't you?'

'Yes, I am, but there's no trouble,' he said.

He had got back into the car where Lesley was waiting and had driven back to see Charmian.

'We should be able to find them even if they are touring,' he said.

'Yes.' Charmian felt sad. Elizabeth Siddons or Phyllis Jones or whatever her name was with parents in South Africa. Nice people, nice girl, if wild. 'Felicity Harrie seemed parentless too, her mother a widow, now living in Canada.'

'She had a grandfather though.'

'So she did, we ought to ask more questions of him. You can do that, Rewley. And get her file out and see what the earlier investigating team turned up.'

'A lot of the work was done by Arthur Grimble,' said Rewley in an expressionless voice. He had not a great opinion of Inspector Grimble, known as Groaning Grimble among the locals. 'Did Lesley go out to Merry-wick with you?'

'Yes, I took her home on my way here,' he looked seriously at Charmian. 'I always take her home first.'

'Go away with you,' she said. 'I know you're laughing at me.' She picked up her phone, preparatory to passing on the information about the Siddons-Joneses to the unit better equipped to find them.

'As if I would, ma'am,' said Rewley, from the door, even more seriously.

*

No sooner had he gone than Charmian's mobile rang. Dolly Barstow, perhaps, or one of the white witches, they had been rather quiet lately. Or Dr Harrie, yes, certainly she wished to speak to him. But it was an unexpected voice which she had to try to remember.

'Greenham here.'

'Oh, Dr Greenham,' she repeated, 'how are things?'

'Well, you will be glad to know that I am not going to sue you.'

'Were you going to?'

'I considered it for a while. But since my daughter is not going to have an abortion—'

'Was she going to?'

'She threatened us with it. But she is not pregnant and never has been. It turns out she is a virgin. Remarkable, isn't it?'

'I have heard of such cases,' said Charmian with careful irony. Was he drunk? No, she decided, it was just a touch of academic hubris. She had met it before. He hoped to shock her. Was she shocked? Yes, she thought she was, a little.

Dr Greenham was talking on, 'Her idea of punishing us, me and her mother. Which she has done a bit.' He stopped talking for a second. 'But that's not why I am ringing. First, it's to say that Fiona has admitted that she went to meet this girl who was murdered. Do you know her identity yet?'

Charmian remained silent.

'I'll take that as a no. Well, Fiona went to meet the girl to get some drugs . . . E, I think, but she's being deliberately vague.'

This time, he was quiet, waiting. Perhaps for praise. She was beginning to see exactly what Dr Greenham was and she was beginning not to like him very much. He was the most boring sort of academic: the sort who is pleased with himself. Or herself. Sex did not count.

Charmian said, bleakly, 'We have found out that the girl dealt in drugs, or pretended to.' Her own feeling was that it was an act. 'It might have been why she was killed.'

'It's to say that Joan Dingham has been with me for an hour and although I don't like her, I think she is going to be a good student.' Another moment of thought, then he said, 'She's clever.' He sounded surprised.

There it was again, that touch she didn't like. Why shouldn't the woman be clever?

'I thought she might be,' Charmian said.

'I don't know how she'll stand the course though, she mayn't have the staying power. You haven't met her yet? No, she mentioned it.'

Charmian thought about her diary and invented an entry. After all, Inspector Parker had invited her. 'I am meeting her and her sister tomorrow.'

'At her sister's place, I bet . . . She's very wary about going around. Can't say I blame her. You might see me there.' He rang off.

No sooner was the phone quiet than Dolly Barstow rapped on the door and was in the room before Charmian could open her mouth.

'Anything new?' she asked hopefully, but the look on Dolly's face did not suggest that there was.

'No. Nix. Nul. Glitz. No progress.'

'Right.'

'The local CID lads say the same. Not getting anywhere.'

'I do get a daily report,' observed Charmian mildly.

'Sure. You get the facts. Or lack of them. I get the emotions.'

Charmian knew that Dolly had a good acquaintance among all ranks of the local CID, and also the uniformed men.

'They tell me what they feel,' said Dolly. 'Bloody low spirited.'

'Is that what you came to tell me?' Charmian picked up her pen with a view to hinting that if so, could she please be allowed to get back to work.

'No, not altogether, but my pal Sergeant Palmer says they feel you and me and SRADIC ought to stay close to what we are supposed to do and leave CID to get on with it. He exempts Rewley. I suppose that's because he's a man.'

'Glad to hear it,' said Charmian tartly.

'Had you wondered? I have a bit sometimes, but you never know with the reserved types.'

'Are you drunk, Dolly?'

'No, of course not. Well, maybe just a bit, I've been really fed up one way and another.'

'Is this a way of telling me you are resigning?'

Dolly Barstow stopped short. 'No, sorry, I apologize, I am being a bit of a wimp. No, I have got some days off due to me, you know we never take the lot in SRADIC.'

'Quite right,' said Charmian, who was beginning to feel in an unforgiving mood.

'But I wanted to ask if I could have a day's leave to go to London. Just twenty-four hours or so. Something personal to sort out.'

Sex rearing its ugly head, Charmian thought. No, delete ugly, why should not the girl have what she clearly wants. I hope it works out. She said so.

Dolly gave her a suddenly radiant smile. 'Well, I think it might. Thanks. And by the way, Palmer said they were sending someone to South Africa to interview the girl's parents and get them back. Jones or Siddons is the name.'

'Information I sent to them,' said Charmian. 'Oh, by the way, when you're in London, you might get out of some of those high London CID men you seem to get on with so well what they know about Rhos Campbell. Yes, I know it was a long while ago and they were lads in knickerbockers, but find out what you can. Thanks.'

They parted on reasonably good terms.

On her way home, Charmian went to call on the witches. They irritated and amused her, but in times of stress, such as now, she found them comforting company.

They were still sitting at their tea table, a well laden one, and at once generously offered her tea.

'Birdie will make a fresh, hot pot,' said Winifred, Birdie's friend and manipulator, or so she seemed sometimes to Charmian.

Birdie looked up to show a spark of that independence which flashed out at intervals to contradict all Charmian's judgements.

'The girl's exhausted, can't you see? Whisky is what she needs, not tea. Come to think of it, I could do with one myself. Produce it, Winifred, you're the whisky girl.'

'Right-oh,' said Winifred, showing no anger.

'I'm not sure,' began Charmian.

'Oh, fiddle,' said Birdie, who was clearly on a high.

She soon communicated why. 'I had an *éclairissement* today.'

Charmian thought about it. 'What is that Birdie?'

'It's when the skies suddenly open and you see through them. As it were,' she added cautiously.

'So what did you see?'

In a practical voice. Birdie said, 'I saw why people dye their hair.' After a pause, she added thoughtfully, 'Or wear a wig.'

Charmian touched her own hair. But no, at the moment it was its natural reddish brown. Might need more help one day but not yet.

'Why do they?'

'To hide,' announced Birdie, with the air of one delivering a great truth.

The arrival of Winifred with a silver tray, several cut glass tumblers and a bottle of whisky interrupted them.

'Drinkies here.'

She, too, sounded cheerful so perhaps she had had an illumination from the heavens as well. But no, her happiness was more financial. As she raised her glass, she said, 'Drink to crime, witchcraft and magic . . . The bookshop turned in a lovely profit this month.'

'You didn't tell me,' complained Birdie.

'You've got a mind above money, I manage money matters.'

'And very well too,' said Charmian politely.

'You can say that with knobs on.' Winifred when particularly buoyant was apt to go back to the idiom of her school days. She took a swig. 'Good idea of yours, this booze. Drink up and we'll all have another dose.'

Charmian tried to protest, but Winifred went on. 'I

think we might go back and live over the shop again . . . We'll exorcise all the ghosts.'

There had been some terrible discoveries the year before when their shop had first been opened. It was in an old house which was built on land of even greater antiquity. In an ancient tomb in the garden had been found old bones, Roman or early British, who knows, except the archaeologists, still pondering the problem. But in with these bones a newer dead body had been found and this body had interested the police greatly.

'I think the gods want us to return,' pronounced Winifred.

The gods usually did line up with anything Winifred wanted, Charmian had noticed.

'Which particular god did you have in mind?'

Winifred nodded her head over her whisky thoughtfully. 'I have considered that matter, and I think Jove . . . It was a Roman site, after all.'

'Thought to be,' put in Birdie, coming to life. She had a taste for the early Celts.

'Of course,' said Winifred, 'I name Jove, but all are just manifestations of the great godhead.'

'I've never fancied Jove,' said Birdie.

'He's also Juno,' Winifred explained, 'they're all One. I've just explained that.'

'You'd never find any of that lot in Stonehenge,' objected Birdie. 'Now I think the Great Lady of the Woods is the one.'

I must ask them which god they are worshipping when they go to Sunday matins at the chapel in the Great Park. The right to attend there, where the Queen herself went, was carefully restricted and an honour.

But she knew what Winifred would say: that attendance there was a social duty.

Charmian was on her way home when she remembered that she had not asked Birdie what she meant by saying that people dyed their hair to hide.

Hide behind it?

When she got home, she found her husband happily cooking in the kitchen. It smelt like duck which was good as she was hungry.

He was drinking red wine as he worked and he poured her a glass which she accepted with some doubt after Winifred's whisky.

'Humphrey, if I dyed my hair or wore a wig, what would you think?'

'With dark spectacles? That you were about to rob a bank.'

'Seriously, please.'

'That you were going on an undercover operation. And don't play about with that claret, it's a good one, one of my best.'

'I haven't done undercover work for a long while.'

He drank deeply before taking the duck out of the oven, sizzling and brown. 'Or that you were conducting an investigation into corruption in the Met.'

Charmian blinked. 'You're not supposed to know anything about that.'

'I'm a good guesser.'

Later, the duck carved and enjoyed, he said, 'Talking of wigs, I thought I saw your protégée in Marks and Spencer today. She was buying tights.'

'My what?'

'Oh, you know, Joan Dingham, the famous killer now turned student. I knew her face, that nose, not long exactly but unusual. No beauty. Surrounded by a cohort of supporters. Friends, I suppose, or protectors. Now she *was* wearing a wig.'

'I daresay she doesn't wish to be recognized.'

'Can't blame her for that. If she wasn't wearing a wig, then she'd been to the hairdressers and had one of those fly-away jobs.'

Charmian had a sudden picture of a customer of Baby's whom she had seen leaving with a froth of hair. Baby had been standing at the door watching and had given a shrug. 'What she wanted. Poor girl has this big jaw and she thinks the hairdo takes the eye off it. What could?'

So perhaps Joan Dingham felt the same way about her nose.

The image of her husband, shopping in the big store and studying a murderer buying tights was interesting and raised a question or two.

'I think Dr Harrie might have been there too, but I could have been mistaken. I thought I just got a glimpse of him in that big mirror next to the new fashions.'

Humphrey had had a good look round, it seemed.

'Do you go there often?' she asked.

'Where do you think this duck came from? And the sauce to go with it, and that salad you are eating?'

'It is good.' She chewed happily for a moment. And then said, 'Do you often see people you know by the tights and stocking display?'

'Now, now, a respectable gentleman like me can walk past the tights. All packaged anyway,' he volunteered knowledgeably, 'like the bras and girdles, which are up the stairs. It's what I call a sexually neutral shop. Not that Joan is.' And he frowned.

Another illuminating thought. On women, her husband's judgement was sound.

'We all go there for food, I meet my chums there, picking over the packets of salmon. Splendid stuff. I daresay even the Queen has dined off it sometimes without knowing it, or knowing it. She's very shrewd. And then someone like old Johnny M., that old soldier, might tell her. Get a royal chuckle and she knows he hasn't got a bean except his pension.' He poured her some more claret, which, with the whisky already consumed, was going to her head. 'That's one thing you can count on with the royals: they always know who's got what in terms of money.'

He'd had a fair bit of claret himself, she thought. Never mind, she liked it when he was slightly in wine. Looked upon the wine when it was red, wasn't that what the poet said?

'We could leave the washing up,' she said.

Chapter Six

Over her breakfast coffee, Charmian found herself thinking about Joan Dingham. It's time I got to see her, most of Windsor had probably sighted her by now: Humphrey has, and no doubt some of his pals while buying their salmon and chickens. Even Birdie has had a look.

I'm sure Birdie saw her and that's who she meant when she was talking about dyed hair and wigs. And I bet she knew exactly who she was talking about too. She's a canny one. Birdie.

Yes, it's certainly time I had a look at Joanie.

She was dressed and leaving the house when the telephone rang. Humphrey had already departed. 'Driving to London early to miss the traffic. Call me at the Club if you want me,' so there was no one else to answer the phone.

Anyway, there was something in the ring that said I am anxious, I really mean to keep on ringing.

A weak little voice answered her.

'Is that you, Baby?' Charmian asked, although it didn't sound like Beryl Andrea Barker, the confident and bouncy one.

'Yes.'

'What's wrong?' Had she missed an appointment to have her own hair done? But in that case Baby would not ring up in tears, but in a blaze of irritation.

'I think I've got a bug . . . Well, no, it's nerves, really.'

'Nerves, you?' Charmian asked, amazed. Baby was pure steel inside, or so it had seemed. Or perhaps it was brass.

'Oh, yes. Joanie came into the salon yesterday to get her hair fixed and I was terrified.'

'Oh, come on, Baby, you know her.'

'I had met her before, yes, I know that, often, but I've never been really close. Never had to touch her.' There was a little shiver in her voice.

Charmian was silent: would she like touching Joan Dingham, feel the hair and skin of a particularly noisome killer? Hard to say.

'It was all right at first, I was just professional, you know.' Baby's voice was getting stronger already, talk, confession, was what Baby had wanted. 'I didn't make it obvious that I knew who she was. I thought she'd prefer it that way.'

Charmian muttered something, her eye on her watch. Out with it, she was thinking, what's this leading up to?

'Her hair is a very bright yellow, glaring really. I thought she might want me to tone it down. Darken it a wee bit. No, it turns out she dyed it herself in prison and likes the colour she's got. Well, all right, I thought, if you want to look like a canary, you've got the beak for it. She does have a big, ugly nose. She's not pretty.'

'No,' agreed Charmian, 'not from her photographs.'

'Now, her sister is, she's pretty. I've always thought

that was the trouble, she hated being the plain one. Well, who wouldn't?' The voice was definitely in control of itself now.

'You sound better.'

'Yes, it's talking to you. But I haven't told you the worst.'

Get on with it, please. Beryl Andrea Barker, Charmian thought.

'Joan wasn't on her own. She had her sister with her, I style Lou's hair so I guess she recommended me. And there were two other women and a man. One of the women was police, I think. I never got introduced. It was fine at first, I offered Joan a chair in a little recess where she could be private, but no, she didn't mind being public, must get used to it, she said. I wanted to change her style to something smooth, but no, she wanted one of those pulled out in clumps and fly-away styles . . . I could do it, of course, but it wasn't going to suit her . . . She said it was her freedom style.'

There was a pause.

'I got one of my juniors to give them all coffee. I think my staff were wondering who they were.'

'You don't think they guessed?'

'They live in their own world: boyfriends, clubbing, clothes, their own hair, the latest colour of lipstick . . . I don't think they know what goes on in the outside world. Don't read, you see. No, I mustn't be unkind, I've seen them reading *Hello!*'

She paused and took a deep breath.

'Then Di came in. You remember Diana? Diana King.'

'Oh, yes,' said Charmian. 'I remember Diana. How did she come to be there?'

A sigh, as from one put-upon and oppressed, came from Baby. 'She's staying with me. For the moment.'

Charmian waited. 'So what happened then?'

'I had told her not to come into the salon, that she was my guest – God help me, but business is business – and to keep away . . . she can be very disruptive can Diana on occasion. I don't know how she does it, and I don't think it's on purpose. Or not always,' she added thoughtfully. 'It just happens. She's suggested we have one last caper before she goes off.' Baby shook her head. 'And I think she means it.'

'Goes where?'

'Oh, just off.' Baby was evasive. One did not make jokes about death.

Charmian drew in her breath. 'But you wouldn't do it? There were four of you last time you really had a go.' Nor was it a successful operation, but she had no need to say so.

'No,' said Baby slowly and, Charmian thought, doubtfully.

'Don't try anything,' Charmian said, in warning. 'And certainly don't tell me if you do. I don't want to go to prison with you.'

'No, I won't. Even if I wanted to, I wouldn't do it, I can see Diana is dangerous company.'

'She always was,' Charmian reminded her.

'Yes, always was,' Baby admitted. 'More so now.' And she shivered. Somehow the shiver came across the telephone line. 'It was when she came in that Joan became unbearable . . . I mean that: I couldn't bear being with her. I had not finished, I was just holding up the hand glass so she could see the back of her hair, and I saw her face. She was looking at Diana as she came in.'

Looking at a reflection looking at a reflection. What do the laws of physics do to the features observed? Coarsen them? Age them? Certainly distort them. Can you believe what you see? Charmian asked herself.

'I tell you: Joan was murder in a mirror.'

'If looks could kill, eh?'

'Don't joke, I'm telling you, for some reason that I don't know, she hates Diana.'

Aware that the telephone call was a plea for reassurance, Charmian offered it. 'Don't worry, and thank you for telling me.'

'It's a warning.'

'Yes, I got that. I am warned. You look after Diana. Where is she now?'

'Still in bed.'

'She ought to be safe enough there.'

'Yes,' agreed Beryl Andrea Barker.

Humphrey met her at the front door. 'What, not gone yet? I've been out and back again.'

A walk was one of his pleasures, before or after a trip to London all the more essential. 'Thinking time,' he called it. 'Good for the mind, the digestion and the bowels.'

'Saw Birdie,' he went on, 'she seems to have something on her mind. Says she'll be coming to see you.'

'It'll have to be later.' Enough time had been wasted already. She drove first to the SRADIC office to see what urgent paperwork had come in. Some was still delivered by the Royal Mail, some was drummed out through the fax machine. She probably hated those most. Then, these days, there was e-mail to consult. However, her efficient secretaries had sorted it all out into urgent, less urgent and forgettable.

She started on the forgettable because these were the easiest and allowed independent thought while dealing with them: she had long since learnt how to split her mind into two.

So, the bigamist of Merrywick; the fraudster of Cheasey – breeding hermaphrodite bull terriers; the professional widow of Windsor whose husbands were about to be dug up. (That one might have to be regarded as urgent, depending on the forensic evidence.)

Reading quickly, she was also thinking about herself. She was starting to feel that, instead of being, as she had hoped when she took the position, a conduit through which all important issues and cases passed, she was simply a walking register of crime, no more, no less. She had come to the conclusion that her career was a kind of lottery in which she sometimes won a prize and sometimes lost. But I've enjoyed it, she thought with some surprise, all these years, working my way up from humble uniformed constable, yes, I have enjoyed it.

And, another jolt of surprise, it has brought me great happiness with Humphrey. Not my first love, but I hope my lasting one. We come different social worlds but we have melded. There was a long history behind them both. Charmian, the girl from Fife, and Humphrey, the English courtier and aristocrat.

I have, let's face it, been lucky.

Top of the urgent list was certainly the death of the Siddons girl, with which she was already concerning herself, no doubt to the irritation of the local CID with whom she was working in tandem.

Less urgent, but fascinating to her was Joan Dingham. To that file, her secretary had attached a note saying that the meeting or party was scheduled for that very morning. She was expected to attend.

'And I am going. On my way now.'

Joan Dingham was staying with her sister, Lou or Lulu Armour, who was a widow. Lou lived in a pleasant flat in a new block out towards Merrywick (there was money in the family shared now between the sisters) and Pip Dingham lived in a small house very close by.

Coburg Court was new and made up of a central block divided into ten apartments while scattered about the grounds, as if dropped there by a master builder in the sky, were several small houses, like chalets, each with a big ground-floor room and a tiny bedroom above. Toy houses really, for one person, or two willing to live very close.

To the left and shielded by trees was a row of garages.

Pip Dingham had one of the houses and his aunt Lou lived in the big block of flats on the top floor. They were all owned by the university. Pip lived there because it was near the big school where he taught.

Lawns and flower beds surrounded the buildings, all well cared for. As Charmian drove in through the gates and took the gravelled drive to the left towards the garages she saw a gardener cutting the grass.

Not the sort of ambience from which you expected brutal murder to spring but of course Coburg Court had not even been built at the time, and Joan Dingham had been living in Richmond then. So she had had to take a train to commit the Windsor murders. So had Rhos Campbell who had lived in South London. Mustn't forget Rhos. The two had been at school together in Slough and had been friends ever since. There had been hints of a lesbian relationship between Rhosamond and Joan (who might be AC/DC), but no evidence of this was brought forward at the trial. Charmian had learned to be cautious about talk of that sort which came up so often.

As she got out of the car she saw an official-looking man, carrying a clipboard with papers attached, approaching the gardener. She had noticed the gardener eyeing her as she parked her car so she guessed that parking here was for residents only. Or was he just curious to know who she was? Anyway, he was bound to know who Mrs Armour had staying with her and probably found the set-up interesting. Of course, it could be that he was part of the protection team which had been provided for Joan, more to keep the peace than out of love for her. If this was the case, the so-called gardener would know Charmian even if she didn't know him.

The man with the board and the papers was standing by the gardener as she came up, he was sneezing heavily and wheezing.

'One of those colds,' he said, muffling his face in a big white handkerchief. 'Better keep away, miss.'

Charmian, who hadn't been very close, stepped back a pace. 'Can you tell me which is Mrs Armour's flat?' He looked the sort who would know. Got it written on that paper he had pinned to his board, no doubt.

She was right, he consulted it before answering. 'Third floor, that is the top.'

He began to follow her into the hall, still sneezing, giving the gardener a quick nod and an admonition to get on with it. This was not well received.

'You work here?' she asked, professional curiosity operating, as it so often did.

'For the university. Check on paint work, that sort of thing. My firm did the work.'

He handed over a card.

A. C. CHAPPELL

All up-keep work undertaken. Painting, etc.

3, Lower Flood Street, High Windsor.

Charmian took it.

'Where is High Windsor?'

'Other side of the castle, going towards Staines. My own naming. Impresses the customers.' He sneezed again into his handkerchief.

A fanciful fellow, she thought. 'That's some cold.'

'Yes, better keep away, miss,'

She had given the gardener a good look as she passed and it seemed to her that he nodded. A tiny little nod that she did not acknowledge.

There was a lift to the top floor: two doors there, two bells, and she had to choose which one to ring. She was standing, preparing to make a decision, when the door to her left opened.

Emily Agent stood there. 'Hi, ma'am, come on in. Been expecting you. Saw you arrive. Inspector Parker's here already.'

A mixed noise of voices, muted laughter and the clink of glasses floated out of the door towards Charmian.

'Party, is it?'

'Sort of.' Emily held the door wide for her to enter.

Inside the room, she saw Dr Greenham, he was drinking a cup of coffee and holding a glass of something strong in his left hand, and talking with animation to a tall woman with bright yellow hair in a crest, rather like the sort of plumes that decorated the helmet of a medieval knight.

Baby hadn't done a bad job within the terms of her commission; it was not unflattering to the strong-jawed face underneath. It did dominate the nose which, Charmian supposed, was its purpose. She knew the face: Joan, old friend of Beryl Barker and Diana.

It was not Joan's flat but she came forward, hand held out, as if it was. Behind her, hand also held out, came a smaller woman, similar to Joan but younger-looking. This was Lou, the younger sister. Perhaps life in prison preserved you, froze you, pickled you, and you did not age so fast. Both women were well dressed and Joan wore a silk suit, something few were wearing this season, just slightly out of date, bound to happen after decades in prison. You lose your eye for fashion.

Or it might be just the genes, the very genes that allowed you to become a murderer. To dream about killing perhaps, at last to achieve it, more than once too. Then to face a trial, a guilty verdict and to come out looking brassy.

Charmian didn't have to introduce herself to Joan.

'I know who you are: Miss Daniels. I have been waiting to meet you.'

Now why doesn't that make me feel happier? Charmian asked herself, while she took Joan's hand and murmured something. She could not quite use the word pleasure, but she did not find herself recoiling in quite the way that Baby had described. She had, after all, touched the skin of more than one killer in her long career. But there was something unpleasant about Joan's touch. Perhaps because although her fingers were chilly and dry, the palm was damp.

A fanciful idea flitted through Charmian's mind: inside the body she was touching were two people: the one Joan was letting the world see and the hot one she was shutting inside.

Not such a fanciful idea. Joan Dingham was not an easy woman to read.

'Lou or Lulu, I answer to both names,' Lou said as she introduced herself to Charmian as Joan's sister. 'Come in and have a drink: coffee or wine or something stronger.'

Across the room, Charmian saw that a lot of the noise she had heard had come from Dr Greenham being professionally jovial. He was talking to a tall, thin, dark-haired woman whom Charmian recognized as Bee – surname for the moment forgotten – a friend of Beryl Andrea Barker. Bee recognized Charmian, with a hint of resignation. She had been one of Diana's gang members, and remembered Charmian's part in their failure.

Charmian accepted a cup of coffee and declined the wine, aware that she needed a clear head. There was a lot to think about: all criminous.

Bee, Diana, Baby, part of the old gang assembling. Were they planning anything? She didn't think so. They might be playing at it. Surely they wouldn't? Their taste had been for fine jewellery shops of which Windsor had several. Then there were the murdered girls, where she had blundered into an investigation not altogether pleasing to her colleagues in the CID; they were behaving with good manners as always. And there was Emily Agent across the room who, if prodded, would certainly let Charmian know what was really thought about her and about SRADIC. Emily grinned and gave her a small wave. This is a strange business you and I are engaged in, the wave and the grin seemed to say.

Perhaps I am being fanciful myself, Charmian thought, for the moment anchored to Joan who was talking away nervously about how happy she was to have this chance of university study.

'Of course, I have to be passed as up to it,' she said.

'You will be, Joan,' said Lou. She turned to Charmian. 'Your friend Beryl Barker is my hairdresser too. Joan went there.' She looked proudly at her sister.

Charmian nodded. 'I know.'

Joan touched her hair. 'She did a good job.' Her hair was bright and flamboyant. Also firmly set with lacquer, it would not wave in a wind, but might be difficult to sleep on.

Hair to hide behind, had been Birdie's view of such display.

'I want to do this work well . . . Perhaps write something. Explain myself.' She turned to her son Pip, who had come up to the three women to offer them wine.

He said gently, 'I don't know, Mum.'

'Perhaps better to leave it alone? You see, I don't know how to behave now I am outside . . .' Joan was nervous. 'Of course, I am going back, but I shall be out and I want people to understand it was not all me.'

She looked at Charmian.

'Joan has never talked about it before, never explained,' said Lou. 'Now she wants to.'

'It might be hard to explain,' said Charmian. 'Can you do it? What will you say?'

Joan licked her lips, which looked dry and hot. She did not answer. Then she muttered, 'I will say that no one is alone.'

Once again, Charmian had the impression that a third person had been involved. A third person besides Rhos?

'Calm down, Mum,' said Pip.

Charmian liked him, she liked Lou, who looked as though this party, if you could call it that, was beyond her powers of control.

'Some sherry?' Lou enquired hopefully of Charmian.

'No, thank you.' Charmian went to the window to look out. There was the man with the board. 'Lovely view.'

'Who is that man?' asked Joan, looking over her shoulder.

Pip approached them to take a look. 'Oh, that's Mr Chappell. He keeps us all in order.'

'Come and meet the person who is helping me.' Joan led Charmian up to Dr Greenham.

Dr Greenham did take some more sherry and gave every indication of having had some, perhaps too much, already.

'She'll make the course,' he said, as soon as Joan's back was turned. 'She's clever enough. But I don't know what to make of her. But who does? She says she is going to write a book "explaining", God help us.'

'She told me that too.'

'She'll get a publisher. TV and newspaper offers too, I guess. She says she had another ex-con who wanted to work with her, but the woman wanted to exploit her.

She's against being exploited. So she sent her away with a flea in her ear.'

'It was a woman?'

'Seems so. They met in prison. Could be a prison visitor, or a warder, I suppose. Or a woman copper.' He looked at Charmian.

'Not me,' said Charmian coldly.

'Evil, the woman called Joan. I must say that I wouldn't care to be her, bearing in mind Joanie's past record.'

He held out his hand for a refill of sherry. Pip poured him some and then moved on to where his mother stood. 'Had a talk with another of them,' he nodded to where Pip was talking to his mother and another woman. 'That one over there. She's been in stir.'

'They don't call it that now,' she said curtly.

'Clink, nick, quod, behind bars. I must go into the etymology of it.' He stumbled over the last long word.

'I'm off,' Charmian said to Pip as he came over. 'Say goodbye to your mother and aunt for me.'

She waved to them both and included Emily Agent in the gesture. Emily seemed stuck, but it was her duty to stay with Joan. Parker seemed to have escaped.

'I'll see you down,' said Pip.

'I can manage.'

'Be glad of the air . . .'

In the lift, as it sped down, he cleared his throat nervously. 'Bit of a cough. Infection, I think.'

'There's a lot of it around,' said Charmian, thinking of the sneezer in the grounds.

'She can't help it, you know. Mother, I mean. She says she needs rewiring . . . It's the years inside. Some of it was spent in solitary because she was afraid of being attacked . . . She wouldn't talk about it.' He meant the killings. 'I don't think she could . . . it was a sort of mutism. Kids get it, I believe, after trauma . . .'

'You were only a child yourself when it happened.'

'Oh, yes,' he agreed. 'Aunt Lou brought me up.'

Mr Chappell was there on the grass.

'Found it all right, did you?' he asked Charmian.

'Yes, thank you.'

As Charmian got into her car, Inspector Parker appeared from another car.

'You got away?'

She nodded. 'Call it that, if you like.'

'What do you make of her?'

'Not sure.'

'I can't believe she did all that killing on her own.'

'She didn't. There was the other woman, the one who killed herself, Rhos Campbell.'

Parker nodded. 'She must have been the dominant party. I'd like to know more about her. I tried to get Dingham talking but she went dead silent. Then I tried the sister. She wouldn't say much either. They specialize in not talking, that pair. The boy talks more, but knows nothing. Just a kid then. Interesting and terrible position to be in, to know that your mother killed other children. What protected him from the same fate?'

'She was his mother.'

'The blood tie? Doesn't always work out, look at the Wests. The family was just easy fodder for them.'

She thought she would chance a probe. 'Anything new about the dead girl found near Threadneedle Alley?'

'Not that I've heard,' he said discreetly. 'But I might not hear. You never get much out of Tim Wibley.'

Inspector Wibley was famous for his buttoned-up lips. 'But you're dealing with that affair, aren't you?'

'Not entirely. It's just that Dolly Barstow somehow got into it at the beginning.'

'And when Dolly gets her teeth into anything, she doesn't give up easily.'

'No.' Unless she's caught up in a complicated love affair which seems to be the case at the moment.

She was not going to tell him about her idea that somehow the death of two girls, one on Pinckney Heath and the other in the scrap of rough land in Windsor itself, was connected with the Joan Dingham killings.

Chapter Seven

When she got back to her office, she asked her secretary to ring the Police Record Office and get her the file on Rhosamond Campbell.

'Now what did you make of that meeting this morning?' she asked herself. 'You have now met Joan Dingham, her sister and her son.'

Murderers, so she had been trained to think, came in three categories: organized killers, disorganized killers and a third category which she had formed for herself.

Organized killers target victims, having chosen the type they fancy; they watch the victim, observing his or her behaviour patterns. This type of killer stalks the victim, choosing the right place and time to do the killing. Such a killer uses a trick or con to get the victim under his control.

The disorganized killer does not choose his victim: if he or she was in the mood it just happened to whomever chanced along. A bad-luck killer, you might say, often choosing a victim at risk to himself. His motive for killing is often a mystery even to himself.

The third category of killer was, to Charmian's mind, better called the theatrical killer. They wanted to make a show, capture an audience. Jack the Ripper would fall into this group. She thought that Joan and Rhos might be killers of this sort. Theatrical killers are a sub-group of the organized murderers, but more controlled. They sometimes hover around the police investigation, watching with pleasure. Years may elapse between their killings, and then the curtain will go up again. All three types of killer may kill more than once, as the mood takes them.

It was her opinion that the killer of the two girls was of this third type, and that he had just opened the show again: the curtains were drawn.

She pushed the papers on her desk away from her and went to stand at the window to look out. Her thoughts were getting complicated. Where does this all lead? Was it coincidence that just when Joan came out of prison a theatrical killer appears on the scene, using some of the symbols earlier used by Joan and Co? Or was it possible that there had been a third killer involved with Joan and Rhos all the time, and that this killer is out and walking around?

Deep breath here, Charmian, she told herself. This is murky water in which you could drown.

Her secretary, Edith, came in with some letters for her to sign. 'There's been a brutal murder in Staines: a stabbing. Woman with her dog.'

'What about the dog?'

'Also stabbed but surviving.'

'Oh, well, Staines is out of my area. It won't come my way,' said Charmian.

'Don't count on it. The woman had a lover who lives in Cheasey.'

Charmian groaned. 'I shan't touch it.'

But she knew she might have to. As head of SRADIC

she was obliged to collect all records, check and observe, and take action if necessary. She had been put there to oversee, a kind of judge of operations who could and did interfere. But the police are very territorial, and her powers only operated within certain boundaries.

As an overseer, she was valued but not loved.

'Has the file I wanted been delivered?' All the records of investigations going back five decades were kept in a barn-like structure at the back of the main SRADIC building.

Any records earlier still were in an underground set of rooms underneath the old police college in Abbey Street, now used as police lodgings for first-year recruits. Anything earlier than that was regarded as a historical document into which not even Charmian Daniels would want to pry, and so these were wrapped in plastic and forgotten, binned. Pre-history. They were tucked away in a vault beneath the old Central Police Station where it was assumed they would crumble away if the rats did not get them first.

'Being sorted,' said Edith. 'Goes back to before SRADIC was started so it's a bit of a muddle, but we will get it.'

'For God's sake get on to it, give them a push.' Her voice was sharp, sharper than she usually allowed herself to be.

The telephone rang and Edith took her chance to escape.

'Charmian? It's me.'

'Yes, I recognized you,' said Charmian with resignation. She had half expected a call from Baby. 'And yes, if you are asking, I did see Joan today, and no, I didn't warm to her, rather the reverse. I liked her sister better and the lad Pip. He had good manners anyway.'

'Yes, Lou's all right, not a bad sort. I don't know how she came to have a sister like Joan. But no one's perfect.'

'You know them,' she persevered. 'Do you think Lou knew what was going on back then?'

'Well, of course,' said Baby. 'Course she did.'

She could be wrong, she often was, but she was a shrewd guesser, born, she claimed, out of being a hairdresser, which taught you a lot about human nature.

'Thanks for that, I'll bear it in mind,' Charmian said, finishing the conversation.

I wish Dolly was here with her own brand of common sense, she can be candid and earthy but she gets it right, Charmian thought to herself.

Rewley banged on the door and walked in.

'I hear Dolly has fled the country with a handsome CID chap from London.'

'Rubbish,' Charmian was abrupt. 'She's gone to London to see what she can get on Rhos Campbell.'

'That's not what the tale is down below.'

'Well, shut them up.'

'Oh, I did. I said Dolly would never elope without telling me.' He rubbed his chin. 'I don't think they believe me.'

He produced a dark parcel from under his arm. 'Edith asked me to give you this. I don't think she cared to handle it too much. Can't say I blame her. It smells. Also, I think she wants to keep out of your way.'

Charmian grabbed the file and confirmed that it was the one she wanted. It looked as though it had spent the last decade in a dustbin. 'I was a bit short with her. Still I've got what I want.'

She turned to Rewley. 'So what did you come to see me about?'

'You've heard about the woman killed in Staines?'

'Yes.' A short answer and a bleak one.

Rewley knew what she meant. Personally, he wanted to move in on this case because the woman had been brutally treated and he was against this. But he could only move if Charmian did.

'It seems as though the boyfriend did her in.'

'Not in our area,' she said. 'Nothing to do with us.'

'Cheasey is though, he comes from Cheasey. And he's gone missing. May be in the Windsor area. In the Great Park.'

'I shall ignore him. Let him stay missing.'

'He's called Charlie Rattle . . . you remember that name. You put his father away. For killing his mother.'

Charmian looked down at her hands in her lap and plaited her fingers. She remembered the murder of Edna Rattle, and she remembered her killer, he had been called Charlie Rattle too.

'Runs in the family,' she said.

A nasty killing it had been too, brutal and messy. Not that Edna had been a delight as a woman: into drink, drugs and on the game.

'But not my business unless asked. And I haven't been asked. And don't you go looking to be asked.'

'Well, you did want to be kept informed. Always. You said advance information was invaluable.'

'Oh, go and emigrate,' she said, and then, as he went to the door, added, 'And before you go, get the details of the latest family game of the Rattles.'

Then she turned to the file of papers which Rewley had brought: it smelt of dust and something that might be mice, because it was wrapped in stained brown paper and tied up with string, both of which looked chewed.

'Needs surgical gloves to handle this safely,' she muttered. 'No wonder Edith didn't care to touch it.'

She cut the string, then folded back the paper. Inside was a dark cardboard folder. It was a thin affair, not packed with papers.

'That probably represents the part Rhos played, or anyway how the police saw her: the supporting player.'

The folder opened stiffly as if no hand had touched it for decades. A dried, flattened fly was on the top page.

She found herself feeling sorry for Rhos: doubly dead and buried with a fly.

She shuffled through the papers, using her fingertips. Before her were the broken shards of the investigation into Rhos's part in the murders.

Four girls had been killed, in groups of two, so only two episodes. The girls had been friends, and in each case they had been out together when they had disappeared.

One pair, Rosy Ridge and Pat Bacon, both aged fourteen, had been swimming and were cycling home together. Their cycles had been found, neatly parked and neatly padlocked outside a small park on the outskirts of Merrywick, on the Cheasey side. The two girls had been killed in the same way, stabbed several times, in the park itself.

The other pair: Susan Meridan and Margaret King, twelve and thirteen respectively, had been walking home together from school in Windsor. They lived near each other but were not otherwise close friends. They were killed in the same way as the first pair – stabbed many times. Susan and Margaret lived in Merrywick but in the only area that could be called poor. They were found side by side, in a half torn-apart old bus in a used-car lot near their homes.

Charmian tried to visualize the scenes, but she had to remember that in the decades since these deaths, there had been a great deal of building which had changed both Merrywick and Cheasey. She knew, for instance, that the area in which Susan and Margaret had lived and died, then not prosperous, had now been completely rebuilt with a large luxury apartment house and a hotel. The used-car lot had long since gone.

A symbol, something between a star and a cross, had been incised with a sharp knife on each girl. The first two girls, Rosy and Pat, had been marked, but less clearly, as if the killer was just learning how to do it. There was a photograph of these carved symbols: on the upper arm in Rosy's case, and on the buttocks in Pat's. Charmian saw that it bore a remarkable resemblance to the marks on the bodies of the two present-day victims.

Peculiar. Was it coincidence? She could not believe it.

Distantly, she could hear a voice saying, 'Who would have seen the original cut and remembered it?'

The answer was any of the police team who had seen the bodies, the pathologist who had examined the victims, and the killer. Oh, and anyone who had seen the photographs if they appeared in any newspaper. She must check on that possibility. Nor could the families of the four girls be ignored.

She picked up the telephone. 'Rewley? Oh good, I want you to check on the newspapers of the time when the four girls were killed and see if the symbols they were marked with were reproduced in any of them.'

'Right,' he accepted his mission without enthusiasm.

'Shouldn't take long, and don't forget local newspapers as well as the nationals. When you've done that, try and locate the families and see if anyone there saw the symbol.'

'That might take some time.'

'Yes, depends how many you manage to locate. Don't spend too long on it.'

Rewley promised with feeling that he would not.

'We will leave the police team and the forensic people and the doctor who would have seen the cuts till later. I am not convinced they could have anything to do with these two new killings.'

'I'm glad about that.'

'But possibilities have to be ruled out.'

As Rewley passed through the outer office, he muttered quietly but so he could be heard, 'I think our respected boss is trying to drive me mad.'

Edith looked up. 'Oh, Miss Daniels wouldn't do anything like that . . . but she has been a bit twitchy lately.'

'Perhaps it's herself she's driving mad.'

Edith looked shocked.

'Just joking.'

'Of course, I knew you were, Inspector.' She nodded. 'I never take any of you seriously.'

Charmian had opened her door and heard this. 'Don't you now? Well, take this seriously: get all the papers in here photocopied for me, I can't bear the smell or touch of them. Then bring them back soonest.'

She shut her door and made herself a cup of coffee. But it wasn't the smell or the dry crumbly touch of the paper that repulsed her, it was that everything she had read created a vivid picture of those four girls as they died.

It was a horrible scene, truly shocking.

And through it all she could see Joan's face, smiling in her cloud of bright yellow hair, and behind her, not smiling but staring through the hair, was Rhos.

She drank the coffee and by the time the cup was empty, she had admitted to herself that neither Rewley nor Edith had been entirely wrong. Twitchy wasn't a bad word.

'I cannot enter into the mind of the killer,' she said aloud. 'But I must stop him entering into mine.'

By the time Edith was back with the original documents and the copies, Charmian was able to smile.

Edith looked relieved. 'Couldn't help reading a bit here and there as I worked,' she said. 'Strange young woman. I mean weird, very weird.'

'You're ahead of me.' Charmian remained amiable. Edith was new in the job, and naive, to reveal that she read what she photocopied. Of course she did, Charmian knew this, but better not to say so.

She picked up the folder of papers. The first document was the first interview with Rhos, which had obviously been conducted formally. Just the usual, regular line of questioning. Clearly the police had nothing on Rhos and were just fishing around. Yes, she knew Joan Dingham. They were old friends. No, she did not know any of the girls who had died, nor could she understand how her name came into it.

Very little was established at the first interview. In the next, she agreed that she had been seen walking in the park where the girls, Rosy Ridge and Pat Bacon, were later found dead. But she often walked there. So did many people. Yes, she knew where the used-car lot was, not far from where she lived and she had probably walked the dog there more than once. No, Susan Meridan and Margaret King were not known to her. Did Joan Dingham go on these walks with her? They were friends, no answer beyond that. Yes, she had bought a sharp knife in the local hardware shop: Kitchen Devil it was called. The purchase had been made several weeks before the murders.

That would be the knife that later turned up in Joan's garage, Charmian told herself. In her car, and stained with blood. The blood of both girls. One of the key features of the case against Joan.

No, Rhos said, she had no idea what had become of the knife. Knives came and went, didn't they? One of the policemen conducting the questioning, Sergeant Mack, had said that not in his kitchen they didn't.

He probably should not have said this because after that Rhos ceased to answer questions. Mutism set in. It had probably already set in for Joan, who had been questioned earlier.

Charmian read on, she could see the case that the police had gradually assembled against the two women.

Both Joan and Rhos had been seen near the sites where both sets of bodies had been found. Joan's car had been parked not far away on the night of the first killing, and had been noticed by another car owner, who had resented it being in the road where he lived, and who had taken the registration number down. The same car could have been in the neighbourhood at the time of the second killing but this time there had been no sharp-eyed cross observer, just a woman out with her dog who thought she might have seen it. Only might, nothing concrete there.

There had been several other questioning sessions, all conducted according to the rules, with Rhos and her solicitor and no answers forthcoming.

It was obvious to Charmian that several other likely suspects would have been undergoing questioning at this time, but that Rhos's silence would have sharpened the feeling against her.

A search of Joan's house had turned up the knife and, hidden in the attic, they had found bloodstained clothes. A jersey was identified by a neighbour as belonging to Rhos.

Charmian raised her head from the papers. She could see the police reasoning: two nicely dressed women could accost the girls in public without raising any fears. Probably they had spoken to the girls earlier, creating a friendly relationship.

But what had been crucial in fixing the murders on to Joan and through her on to Rhos were two facts that had been carefully kept from the press. One girl had had her nails painted a vibrant silvery green, while the other wore a soft pretty pink. The other pair had been scented with an expensive new scent called Diorama and one of them had the nail on the little finger of her left hand painted purple.

In Joan's house they had found a small beauty pouch with several bottles of nail varnish, coloured from green through pink to purple. There had also been a small selection of scents, of which Diorama was one. These were the sophisticated sweetmeats which had lured four teenagers of the seventies to their deaths.

Next, Charmian found a photograph of Rhosamond

among the papers. A plump ordinary-looking young woman wearing big spectacles – this style had just begun to be fashionable about that time, Charmian remembered – her hair, long and curly.

Not a face you would notice or think about after you had left her.

Charmian turned the photo over. On the back Rhos had written: 'To us from Rhos'. No message, no date, and possibly the photograph had never been given to its intended recipient, since here it was in the archive.

Who was 'us'? she asked herself. Probably Joan and Rhos.

Beneath the photograph was a small, blue book. Inside was a diary.

It was a diary of very short handwritten comments, scrawled comments. No dates except for the names of the days. It seemed to be from the last week or so of Rhos's life. The book had been immersed in water and passages were obscured, turned into blue patches where the ink had run.

Sunday

Not a holy day nor holiday except for some. The police for instance. No questioning today. I would keep my silence, of course. As told to. Sometimes, I begin to question my docility. But I have been . . . so long now, and got pleasure and given pleasure, accepted advice if not orders, that I do not know if I can change now. What I . . . cannot . . .

Monday

Start of a new week, Feels like the old one. Not good. I can't get through to Joan . . . Fear . . . But I have

been told what to do. As always, I do it. Where is
the joy, where is the pleasure? It is all gone . . .
Revolting . . . There has to be a way out.

Tuesday
Police day. I say nothing.

Then a splodge of text where the water had made the ink run.

Charmian could make out the word: pain. Pain was part of a sentence the rest of which was lost. 'Whose pain?' she asked herself.

She could make out nothing more of this entry. The paper was very fragile and there were several holes.

Wednesday. This had been a densely written page but the ink had run creating a pale blue wavy pattern. But here and there was the shadow of a sentence.

Charmian thought she could read – I have been used . . . Joan . . . She . . . The name Joan was clear enough, but she, or was it he?

There was not much more to be got out of Wednesday but Thursday was clearer.

By Thursday, Rhos was letting her feelings run wild. Once again that phrase: I am used . . .

Charmian frowned. Not easy to read. Might be, just possibly might be: I am abused, Rhos's writing was unclear.

In the middle of the page of indecipherable scribbles one sentence stood out.

I have been used, instructed, taught, I can do no
more . . . they must be on their own.
I cannot go on.

Another set of words stood out: the Great Park . . . and then the lake was mentioned a few words on. The words in between could not be deciphered. At the bottom of the page were the words: I shall have to say.

What she was going to say was unknown.

That was the lot. After this a whole block of pages had been torn out. By whose hand, she could only guess. But she was beginning to make guesses.

The next piece of paper that interested her was the account of Rhos's death. She had been missing for several days before her body had been found, caught in weeds in the lake in the Great Park. One of the park rangers had found her, half hidden by all the greenery.

The police surgeon's report settled for suicide. The inquest on her had produced a verdict of death by drowning. There was a contusion at the back of her head, probably caused as she jumped in. The lake was not that deep, but you can drown anywhere if you put your mind to it.

She had left no letter. No signs that she was preparing to depart this life were to be found in the small neat flat she lived in. She had travelled by train from Richmond to Windsor, then walked to the park. She had travelled first class, the ticket was in her pocket. Her handbag, with the diary in it, was later dredged from the bottom of the lake.

By this time, Joan was already under arrest. She did not comment on the suicide of her friend. She smiled sometimes, kissed her sister when she visited, but hardly spoke to her, and to the police not at all.

Mutism was operating.

Oddly enough there was a photograph of Joan in the file. A much younger Joan, hair not so puffed up and yellow, just falling about her face in a natural way. She had a half smile. Across the bottom she had written: Love From Joan.

Charmian closed the folder and walked to the window to look out. She looked in the direction of the Great Park. She imagined that she could just see the tops of the trees. The Great Park, the old hunting ground of the Norman kings, stretched all around Windsor, Merrywick and Cheasey. They had hunted for pleasure but also to eat, since the enormous royal household needed the venison that they killed.

'Nice old world, full of killers.' Charmian said aloud. She turned away from the window. 'And they are my job, my career has been built around them and on them, so what does that make me?'

A kind of partner.

Then her good sense reasserted itself: she was doing a job that had to be done, and which she did well. It was the theatrical element to these murders that was getting to her.

She picked up the file and a small piece of paper fluttered out. On it was drawn, in thin pencil lines, the symbol between a cross and a star which had been cut into the girls' skin, and which she thought she had seen again in the latest victims.

Underneath was written: Our Sign.

Not so far away, in London, by the Thames, Dolly Barstow had enjoyed a very satisfying quarrel and then a reconciliation with her former lover, a high-ranking police officer and much married man. All this had been gratifying to Dolly since she had scored a great number of points in her quarrel speech (it had been a speech, carefully prepared by her and delivered in a formal manner while standing erect) after which the reconciliation had been on her terms which meant she had control.

She was offered, and refused, a plan for marrying. 'Not likely,' she had said. 'How many divorces would that make for you? And me next on the list?'

Not kind of her, but she was not trying to be kind, or even, it must be admitted, honest. She was acting, but it was time, she thought, for a woman to stand up for herself.

She had then got her hair cut, bought some new shoes of a style not to be found in Merrywick and joined a few friends for a drink in a carefully chosen bar.

The conversation had been interesting.

She was staying with an old college friend. Amanda Deacon. A lawyer. Amanda had a flat in a converted warehouse where she lived a hardworking even austere life: no lovers, no drugs, not much drink. She swam every morning and jogged every Sunday. Her intention, as she had stated more than once, was to retire in her early forties and sail around the world in her small boat.

Dolly, who knew that Amanda could confuse Salisbury and Bath, wondered how she would get round the world.

'I can get maps and charts,' said Amanda. 'And I shall take sailing lessons before I go.' She poured them some more wine. Dolly had brought a bottle of Sancerre with her together with a salad and a chicken dish from the deli round the corner from Royal Street where Amanda lived.

'Thank you for having me,' said Dolly.

'You're only here for twenty-four hours.' Amanda was eating placidly. 'You're welcome to stay longer.'

'I wanted to get away. Think things out.'

'And did you?' The legal mind was operating.

'Did what I wanted.'

'And how much actual thinking came into it?'

Dolly protested that you could think in all sorts of ways.

'And positions?'

Dolly poured out some more wine. 'Never you mind.' She added, 'I did some good work too.'

In the bar where she had gone for that drink, she had talked to a group of CID men.

'Picked up something that will interest my boss . . . I think I will have to tell her.'

Charmian was considering packing her briefcase, preparatory to departing for home, when her telephone rang. She considered ignoring it: it had been a long day and she was tired. But the call was on her private, reserved line, a number known only to a few. Among whom, of course, were the white witches.

'Charmian, it's Birdie.' She sounded agitated. 'Could you call on your way home?'

'Something wrong?

'Yes, I fear so.'

Behind Birdie, Charmian could hear Winifred saying, 'Tell her now, why wait, tell her now.'

'No,' Charmian heard Birdie say. 'I want to tell her

face to face. Without seeing me, she may not realize how seriously I take this.'

Charmian didn't wait for any more. With those two, it was better to get things over. 'I'm on my way home now, I'll call in as I pass.'

It was never easy to escape from Birdie and Winifred, they were tenacious in everything they did, social contacts included.

Dr Harrie's mongrel dog was sitting at the door when she arrived.

'Hello, boy.' She patted his head and went through into the hall. 'Birdie, Winifred, I'm here.'

Their house smelt of cooking: vanilla cake, buttery shortbread, something savoury. No doubt a party for fellow witches and warlocks was being prepared. They entertained a lot in a modest way because Winifred held a high position in the Berks and Bucks Coven. Coven was the word used although a more respectable group of ladies could not be imagined. There was one warlock admitted as an honorary member whom Charmian on first meeting had thought, sexually speaking, could as well have been witch as warlock, until Birdie confided in her that he had impregnated two junior witches. The witches approved rather than otherwise, viewing this as almost a function of a warlock. Puritans they were not. In fact, Birdie had even hinted delicately that she and Winifred 'were not totally without experience', although she gave no details. After all, she had added, 'We both served in the Fire Service in the War.'

Charmian went into the kitchen where the ladies of experience sat her down and offered her tea or coffee. 'Or a glass?'

Charmian refused all refreshment. 'Tell me, what is it?'

Winifred said, 'It's Dr Harrie. He's gone.' She pushed a note across to Charmian. 'He left this for us.'

Charmian read:

> DEAR FRIENDS,
>
> THIS IS ALL MORE THAN I CAN BEAR. I MUST BE OFF. DO NOT GRIEVE FOR ME.
>
> PLEASE LOOK AFTER THE DOG.
>
> H . . .

The letter was in staggered printed capitals as if the writer was drunk. There was more to the signature but it could not be deciphered easily, although a capital H at the beginning was clear.

'I'm afraid he wasn't himself when he wrote it,' ventured Birdie nervously.

'No. Not by the look of it.' Drunk perhaps. 'Where was this left?' Charmian asked.

'Pushed through the letter box. No envelope, just folded.'

Charmian nodded. She could see the creases in the paper. 'And the dog?'

'Sitting outside on the mat, waiting . . . We took him in, of course, but he seems to prefer to sit outside. Waiting for his master,' said Birdie sadly.

'Yes, I saw him.'

At that moment, the dog trotted in, disposing himself comfortably in front of the big solid-fuel cooker where the heat was greatest. He was a ragged-coated, rangy beast, with a sharp nose and strong teeth. But he looked good humoured.

Charmian nodded at him and he almost but not quite nodded back.

'It looks as though you've got him for life.'

Winifred said sharply that they would have to think about it.

'I am afraid the poor man may have done away with himself,' said Birdie.

'I don't know about that.' Winifred was still sharp. 'He didn't say so in the note.'

'I fear it was what he meant.' Birdie shook her head. 'I fear he was not himself even when we spoke to him.'

Charmian sat down at the kitchen table to consider the problem. 'I'm not inclined to worry too much. He was roaming round, trying to find out about his granddaughter's death.'

'Murder,' put in Winifred. 'It was murder.'

'Murder,' agreed Charmian. 'I don't think he found anything, I guess he gave up the struggle and has gone home. He must have had a home somewhere, and he is probably there, sitting comfortably in his own house.'

'If only we knew where that was,' said Winifred.

'Shouldn't be too hard to find.'

Even to herself, it sounded unconvincing.

'I think he is in the river,' said Birdie. She passed her hand over her face. Winifred reached out and took her hand. 'Come on, old thing.'

Birdie raised her face. 'I'm not crying for him, Win. It's just that somehow it is all so strange and odd.'

'Don't be frightened.' Her friend put a comforting arm round her shoulders.

'No, but there is a bad feeling . . . I sense it.'

The witches did not lay claim to any extra sensory

perception but it was true that Birdie was more sensitive to the oddities of human behaviour than Winifred.

'I feel something black.'

Winifred patted her friend on the shoulder. 'I'll get you a cup of strong tea, that will buck you up. I am sure the old chap is all right. Whatever you felt about him, I felt he could look after himself.'

'Well, that is true,' said Birdie, slowly as if considering. 'I will have that tea. What about you, Charmian?'

'No, I will go home. Do you want me to report Dr Harrie as missing?'

'I think he will turn up,' said Winifred.

Birdie shook her head. 'You might be right, Win, but I believe it would be best if Charmian did report him missing. I just feel it would be the right thing to do.'

Winifred met Charmian's eyes, she gave a small shrug but said nothing.

'I'll do it. Do you mind if your names come into it?'

'Have to put up with it,' said Winifred gruffly, 'we do come into it. He was staying here.'

'They will want to talk to you, I expect.'

'I wonder if we will see that nice young detective we saw when we had that little trouble in our bookshop.' Birdie was reviving.

Little trouble, Charmian thought, several bodies in their own garden, one at least the work of a mightily unpleasant killer.

'I can't say who will be interviewing you, not my sphere.' Charmian slung her coat over her shoulders. 'Humphrey will be wondering where I am.' Not that she was ever back home at any regular time. 'I'll let you know what I have done and of course anything I learn will come your way too.'

'But they will tell you first,' said the worldly wise Winifred.

The dog followed her to the door, wagging his tail, as if prepared to follow her. Like most dogs he knew how to make a play for sympathy.

'Don't worry, boy,' she said, patting his head. 'You're safe. They won't get rid of you.'

She drove the few yards which separated her house from where Birdie and Winifred lived. She had lived in this early Victorian cottage before she married, and had hesitated before asking her husband to move in with her. It was small, whereas he was used to large rooms in a large house; for a time when they were first married they had shuttled between his various homes. Charmian had even herself bought a country home. But it was no good, she was a town dweller. Fortunately she had never sold her cottage, not even rented it out, so they had moved back in together. To her pleasure and surprise, they were happy there.

Various animals had come and gone in their lives, each creature dying of contented old age, but at the moment Charmian and Humphrey were on their own. A vacancy usually summoned up a replacement, Charmian could not remember ever going out and choosing a cat or a dog, they seemed to choose her.

Her husband appeared down the stairs, spectacles in his hand. He kissed her on the cheek.

'You look thoughtful.'

'How would you like a large mongrel who seems to

have been left on the witches' doorstep by your old school mate, Dr Harrie?'

'He wasn't my mate, not ever, I just knew him, and I didn't recognize him this time round except by name.'

'Perhaps you made a mistake.'

'Perhaps I did. I recall the dog.' He was doubtful. 'I don't know, I like a dog with a breed.'

'Oh, he's got a breed, the trouble is he's got too many, all mixed up. I think he's got character . . . He'd be a good companion for you when you go for one of your long walks.'

Humphrey had what he called his 'thinking walks' when he paced along, considering problems. He was immersed in drama at the moment, writing a short play for the class he attended at the local university. The student body was large, some students living in university residences but most renting flats or travelling daily from their own home. A far call from the groves of academe of the older universities.

Humphrey loved it, though, and said that for someone of his age, it was just right.

He was not so sure about the dog. 'He looks the sort that would chase the pheasants in the Great Park. Eat them, too, I daresay.'

Charmian had to agree. She put down her bag and advanced to the kitchen. The dog looked a cheerful scoundrel if ever she had seen one. 'We've got cold pheasant and salad to eat tonight. I cooked it before I went out this morning.' She was better at cold chicken or ham or pheasant, something you prepared in advance and left to eat later, hot foods, that had to be ready and eaten at a set time or they spoiled, confused her.

'What's happened to old Harrie then?'

'Went off, leaving the dog behind with a request for the witches to look after him. They think Harrie is bent on suicide. The river is their guess.'

'I doubt it, he didn't look that sort.'

'You can't tell,' said Charmian. 'People don't come labelled.'

'I ran across the lad Pip Dingham today . . . Dr Dingham, I should say, he's going to be a lecturer in the university, soon to be Professor Dingham, no doubt. Clever boy. Wonder how he copes with his mother?'

'By ignoring the relationship as much as he can from what I saw. His aunt brought him up so he probably counts her as his mother. But he behaves well, he's polite and kind to Joan. He may even be sorry for her.'

'Think so?'

'I don't know. I must make a call. Lay the table, we can eat in the kitchen.'

She went up to her workroom at the top of the house. 'I'll call John Tincker,' she said to herself. He was uniform, not CID, an Inspector on an accelerated promotion track. He had worked on the periphery of the Pinckney Heath killing.

Briefly she told him about Dr Harrie and his disappearance. 'He may have killed himself. Late middle age, lots of hair still, weirdly dressed. If such turns up, it will be Harrie. But let me know of any unclaimed bodies within that age range.'

'Right,' said Tincker. 'Didn't know there was a grandpa. Only met the mother. She's gone to live in Canada.'

'It might be an idea to check on his home address; he may be there, comfortably drinking a glass of beer.' Charmian suggested.

'Do you know it?'

'I am sure you can find out,' said Charmian sweetly. 'I'll owe you.'

'Oh, I'll call in the debt some time.'

He probably would do, he was punctilious himself, and expected the same back. He had a clever wife who was a neuro-surgeon and a daughter who was certainly intelligent, but at one year old it was a bit early to tell.

'I'll feed it into the system and let you know what comes out.'

Back in the kitchen, she said so little and was so distracted that finally her husband said 'Want to shoot me tonight?'

'Lovely,' she said absently.

'Oh, I'm glad you look forward to it. I want you to enjoy it.'

'Always do.' Then she looked at him. 'Sorry, I didn't hear what you said. I was thinking.'

'I noticed,' he said soberly.

'About those killings that Joan Dingham went down for . . . I did a lot of reading this afternoon – Rhos's diary, various reports. I started to wonder.' She paused. 'Could there have been another person involved as well as Rhos and Joan?'

'You're not asking me?'

'No,' she shook her head. 'I just feel . . . another presence.'

'Not like you.'

'No, I wouldn't say I had a lot of imagination.'

'Oh, you have, but it operates in a very down-to-earth, realistic kind of way,' he smiled at her with admiration. 'That is why you are good at what you do.' He never used the word detection about her work because he thought she was above and beyond that; establishing the truth, he preferred to call it.

Charmian smiled. 'Grateful for your praise.' She reached out her hand to him. At that moment, her mobile phone rang in her handbag on the kitchen floor.

She bent down to pull it out of the bag. 'Dolly, good to hear from you.'

'Just something I picked up in London. Thought it would interest you. Might mean nothing, of course.'

'Come on, spill it out.'

'I was talking to a CID man who was working on the Dingham killings, London did some looking into Rhos as well as Joan. He was very junior then, just become CID, but heard all the gossip, and there always is what you might call drinking gossip. You know that. Well, there was talk of a third person involved. Someone who kept out of the spotlight. I pass it on to you, for what it is worth.'

'Thank you, Dolly. It interests me. Let's talk it over.' She did not say more, except, 'Why was the idea not followed up?'

'Don't know. I guess it was just an idea passed around which came to nothing. And, of course, they already had Joan and there was a lot of feeling against her, so I've heard.'

'That's true.'

'I will be back tomorrow. Early. Back to work.'

Humphrey had refilled her glass. 'Well, I heard that. Dolly's voice would a carry a few streets.'

'Has done,' admitted Charmian with a smile. 'During a crisis.'

Not only Dolly's voice could carry; from outside

there came a bark. A polite bark, but one demanding an answer.

Husband and wife looked at each other.

'Do you hear what I hear?' asked Humphrey.

For answer, Charmian left the kitchen to open the front door.

'Oh, it's you.'

The rough-coated mongrel bowed his head politely and moved his tail. Better not to utter, he had obviously decided, but keep quiet and mind your manners.

She said accusingly to him, 'You followed me round here.'

There was no answer, but if there had been, then it would have been on the lines of: I didn't have to follow, I have known for some time where you live. I always do my homework and I have a good nose. And I know you are a sucker for a fine-looking fellow with a rough coat . . . And talking of smells, that has to be pheasant.

Charmian sighed. 'Come on in. I'm not saying you can stay.'

The dog followed her in, his tail gently wagging. He knew that once in, you were in for good. This was the home for him.

Chapter Eight

When the telephone rang, Charmian was drinking a restorative glass of red wine, and the dog was eating a bowl of carefully boned pheasant.

She knew at once who was calling. 'It's all right, Birdie . . . he's here with us.'

'Oh, I'm so glad he found his way.'

'He did, indeed.' The dog looked up and moved his tail gently before going back to his bowl.

'I don't want you to think we sent him. It was entirely his own idea.'

Charmian looked at the dog. 'I believe you.'

'Of course, we are mainly vegetarian eaters, he may have sensed it.' Yes, he had, decided Charmian.

'What's he doing now?' Winifred took over.

'Eating.'

She put the telephone down and faced her husband.

'I expect we'll all have a very happy life together,' he said. 'That was Winifred, was it? Thought I recognized her voice, there's a metallic overtone that comes across. Not always, but sometimes. I bet she put him up to it. In a witchy way.'

'Oh, I don't want to think it.'

'Go on. They're more ruthless than they look, that

pair.' He eyed the dog's length. 'He's not sleeping on the bed.'

'I don't suppose he'd want to, he doesn't look that sort. I wonder where he comes from?'

'Dr Harrie. They came together.'

'I didn't mean that exactly. Wonder where Dr Harrie got him?' Charmian studied the now sleeping dog. 'Not the sort of dog you go and buy. Animal refuge perhaps. He doesn't look as though he has a high price tag.'

'They may have lived together since he was a puppy.'

'I think they just joined up together and Harrie took him on. Company. Or window dressing.'

'That's a funny thing to say.' Humphrey was just beginning to realize that there was more to this conversation than talk about a dog.

'What sort of a person was Harrie? You were at school together.'

'Just my prepper,' protested Humphrey. 'I hadn't seen him for years. Just saw his name occasionally in the Old Boys' Mag that comes once a year. You always look for the people you used to know.'

'Do you indeed?' asked Charmian, amused.

'It's human nature,' protested her husband. 'Why are you so interested?'

'Let's just see what we get if the man's body turns up.'

'Perhaps he was just joking in his note . . . No. Come to think of it, Harrie wasn't the type to make that sort of joke. He may have wanted to get shot of the dog, although it's a rather underhand way of doing it, and I don't remember him as being like that. No, if he hinted that he was going to depart this life, then that's what he meant.' He shook his head. 'I must say you are taking it very calmly. Can't he be stopped?'

'There is a search under way, we may find him in time.' She finished her wine. 'I've got a bit of paperwork to do. Won't be long.'

She went up to her office where she sat at her desk, turning over the papers in a bright yellow file.

After a while her husband came up the stairs, and up to the desk. He touched her gently on the arm.

'You're worried about the Dingham woman, aren't you? And Dr Harrie, and the two girls who were killed. Not like you, Charmian, you always keep control, don't let things get on top of you.'

'Things are a bit mixed up.'

'No, love, you're just tired. Come to bed.'

'Yes, you're right. I'll just tidy these papers up and then I will.'

'Go and have your hair done tomorrow,' said her husband as he walked away. 'It always helps a woman, that's something I've learned. Noticed it over the years.'

Charmian laughed. It was newly washed but he hadn't noticed that.

'That nice little blonde you go to.'

'Oh, you noticed that too, have you?'

Baby, a nice little blonde? Oh, yes, and many other things besides.

He put his arms round her as she got into bed, she was cold. 'You're cold and shivering.'

'Not now,' she said, hanging on to him.

'What is it?'

'I don't know. Bad thoughts.'

'You're not going to say, are you?'

'No, not yet.'

She began to feel warmer. Sleepily, she said, 'Not hair, nails, I might book myself into Baby's for bright green nails.'

'And if you do, I might throw you out of bed . . . Where's that dog?'

'Asleep in the kitchen.' She was nearly asleep herself now.

Outside, there was a soft pad pad as the dog came up the stairs and disposed himself to sleep outside the bedroom. It was always wise to sleep near to those in charge of household matters. Like food for instance.

He had already worked out who was boss in this house: her.

Baby was always first in the salon in the morning to check that the cleaners had left everything immaculate. She had a good team of workers but experience had taught her that you had to check. Nothing was worse for an early client than to come in and find yesterday's hair left in a basin. And since the salon was not far from one of the local TV stations, there were sometimes very early clients, some of whom Baby saw to herself. One or two of them liked a bit of privacy as well, which was why they came with the dawn and in some cases preferred to be attended to in a curtained alcove rather than in the open room. Both sets, TV or private, of what she called her 'early-morning ladies' were always well informed so that Baby usually knew more of what was being said, rumoured and laughed at even than Charmian.

Joan Dingham had been one of her recent early-morning ladies. Even on her first visit she had declined using the curtained alcove, she had said she had had enough of being closed in, and had had her hair done in the open room.

I may not like you, Baby had thought, and I don't, but you are brave. Tough too, to have done what she had done, lived through the punishment years, and now come out into the daylight. It might be dangerous daylight, there were plenty in the world outside who were full of ill will towards her.

Lou, too, usually came early, but this was because for years she had worked in the offices of a local firm not far from Baby's salon and could have her hair washed and dried on her way to work. She too valued the fact that the salon was almost empty at that time. In the early years she had been shy about showing her face because she was Joan's sister, but she had got bolder.

No one had ever asked Pip what he had endured as the son of a killer, it was simply recognized that he had to endure it. He couldn't hide, life always found you out in the end. So he had survived, treating life cautiously, waiting from day to day to see where it bit next. Baby knew that Lou had supported him through all this and that they loved each other.

'Poor kid has no mother and no father,' Lou said over some coffee as her hair was being dried that morning. 'Not to count, with Joanie in prison and his father off into outer space for all I know, disappeared before he was born. Never seen again. So it's all been up to me.'

'You've done a good job, Lou,' Baby said. Give credit where credit is due was a law with her.

She had to stop then because the phone rang.

'Hello Charmian. Want to make an appointment?'

Lou listened.

'Right, let me look in the book. This morning, about nine. Let me know, if you can, if you have to cancel.' A long acquaintance with Charmian had taught Baby that she often did have to cancel. 'I've got some lovely new colours . . . Yes, I have got green, but I don't think it's quite you.' She went back to Lou. 'People always surprise you, there she is, that lovely lady, no longer quite young, asking about green nail varnish . . .' She shook her head.

Lou looked at her own nails, immaculate but unpainted. 'Prefer natural myself . . . Have you still got Diana with you?'

Baby admitted cautiously that she had. 'Can't turn her out, not yet.'

'What's she up to?'

What she's up to is dying, Baby wanted to say, but instead she just gave a shrug. 'Who knows? Nothing.'

'Oh, come on, you know she's always up to something.'

'Nothing she's told me about.' This was not quite true. Baby passed over their joke about staging a robbery which Diana might have been serious about.

'She's always short of money,' said Lou.

'Yes, but who isn't?'

Lou was silent while Baby put the final touches to her hair, and sprayed it with lacquer. 'She's been in touch with Joan.'

'I thought she had.'

'Joan doesn't like her, and that's an understatement.'

'I don't know why. They've got a lot in common.'

Not something you should say to Joanie's sister, but there, she'd said it.

'Diana told Joan she was going to write a book about her. Her crimes, her guilt and her life. Very publishable. Diana said she was going to include a chapter about herself but it was mostly to be about Joan and Rhos. She said she knew something that had been a secret and she was going to put it in the book. That would be the selling point. It would make a great deal of money.'

'I suppose it would.'

'No suppose about it: serial rights, TV rights, film rights, and possibly foreign sales. Joan was furious . . .'

'Seems reasonable.'

'She was planning a book herself, she wants the money for Pip. It's why she wants to do this university course, so she'll write a good book, not just popular trash. She thinks that Diana chummed up with her when they were inside together for a bit to get information.'

'Sounds like Di,' Baby admitted, there was nothing altruistic about Di. Diana was dying, but she still might want the money. 'Why are you telling me all this?'

'Because Diana says she knows a lot that never came out, more than Joan has ever admitted, and she's going to put it into the book.'

'How could Diana know more than Joan?'

'Perhaps she does know something,' said Lou, 'or she may just have a good imagination.'

'Sounds dangerous,' said Baby lightly.

'Could be. You and I have been good friends, Baby, haven't we?'

Baby nodded without saying anything. Was she a friend?

'I'll tell you something that I wouldn't tell anyone else: Joan is angry but she's also frightened. Think about that and what it means.' She stood up. 'You've got my hair just right. Thanks.' She picked up her bag. 'Look, do try to tell Diana to back off.'

Baby put out her hand and gripped Lou's arm. 'Wait a minute, wait a minute, don't just go. What do you mean?'

'Just warn Diana.'

And Lou was off, out of the salon and into her car. She gave Baby a wave as she drove off.

Baby went back into the salon, heated up what was left of the coffee, then sat down to consider what had gone on. The salon was beginning to fill as more of her assistants came into work, gossiping and laughing, and the first clients arrived. Bobby had the morning off.

'Hello, Megs,' she said as the top stylist hung up her coat and prepared to start work. Megs was christened Cressida but years of being called Mustard and Cress had forced her to change her name.

'Isn't it a lovely day?' Megs was touching up her eyeshadow, red was the new colour this season which gave her a flushed look as if she had been in a fight. She was reputed to be a good fighter and at least one lover had crawled away to nurse a broken nose.

Baby looked out of the window. 'It's raining,' she said morosely.

'I know,' said Megs, 'but I'm happy.' She stared out of the window at the rain, now pouring down with hail as well. 'Fucking lovely, isn't it? Rain on a bare bottom.'

Baby sat up straight and glared at her. Baby was broadminded about what her stylists did in their spare time (she worked them so hard that they had precious little energy left, but Megs had stamina), but at work they were expected to be ladies. Like air hostesses.

'Watch your tongue, Megs.'

'I'll wash my mouth out with hair mousse,' said Megs with a giggle. She wriggled into her pretty grey overall and sped off, favourite ivory-handled hair brush in hand. 'What I do with that brush in my own time is my own business,' she said over her shoulder.

'Mind your step, Megs,' Baby called after her.

She would like to have given Megs notice to leave on the spot (and not for the first time), but Megs was surprisingly popular with many clients, and not, as might have been expected, with some of the men who came in, but with the elderly women. Megs and a blue rinse seemed to meld.

Baby finished her coffee, making the decision to talk to Diana, and then talk to Charmian Daniels when she came in for her manicure. She always found a talk with Charmian restored her sense of humour.

'Laugh at the black patches, girl,' she instructed herself as she went up the stairs to her flat. 'That's what you've always done and that's what gets you through.'

And if it wasn't strictly true, you could always have a good laugh on the way.

'Di?' she called. No answer. Which meant nothing. Diana never answered unless it suited her. She was in the bedroom applying eyeliner. No sign of her packing and going away, Baby noted. In fact it looked more like she was settling in.

'Sorry I couldn't answer. No can do when putting on liner . . . Get it all crooked.'

Baby gave a closer look. 'What colour is it?'

'Gold. I reckon I deserve gold.'

'I heard from Lou that you are out to get gold too.'

Di gave her a sharp look. 'So what did she say? No, don't tell me, I can guess. That sister of hers is paranoid, you know that. Joan's killed before. Do it again, I daresay, if she got the chance. I suppose you can get a taste for it.'

'So you're not going to write a book about her?'

'Is that what Lou said? Joanie will have fed her that line. She hates me, you know. Nothing to do with any book. I'll tell you what it is: where we were, in prison, you had to take sex where you could get it, and I turned her down. She couldn't forgive me.'

Baby looked at the half-made-up face with one eyelid decorated with a hoop of gold and the other naked.

'If you say so.'

'I do say so.' Di grinned. 'And I had better luck than she did. Every single time.'

Baby turned away. 'I never know whether to believe you or not.'

'Oh, come on, love, we're old friends, comrades in arms, you've been good to me.'

Baby sighed and smiled. Di could always get round her. 'Yes, well, look after yourself. Where are you off to now?'

Diana pulled a face. 'The hospital. A session. I do have them, you know.' She added. 'It might take a long time. I might be there all day, you never know.'

'Right, I'll leave the door unlocked.'

'Thanks, Baby. I won't forget how kind you've been. Meet you in the golden wood.'

It was a joke between them. Once, a long long time ago, they had both been in a pantomime. They had been the Babes in the Wood.

'Picking golden leaves off the tree,' rejoined Baby. 'Happy days.'

'Want me to drive you to the hospital, the car's outside? It's quite a walk.'

'Thanks, but no. I want the air.'

Charmian looked down at her nails. Not green. That had been a joke, but something stronger than her usual pale pink.

Later that morning she had a committee meeting in London which for once she was reluctant to go to. Usually she enjoyed meeting some of the other committee members. Even if the meeting itself was dull, which it could be, it was an opportunity to pick up the gossip of the wider scene in London. All information was useful in her job. Today though, Windsor interested her more.

The inquest on the two girls was today. Separate inquests but on the same day. She herself was not going but Dolly Barstow would be there, and probably Rewley as well. She would get back from London in time to hear what had happened. What could be expected was that both inquests would be adjourned to a later date.

She enjoyed the committee meeting more than usual, being initiated to the local story doing the rounds which this time concerned a prominent television presenter, who was reputed to be besotted with his dog.

'What? You don't mean . . .' queried Charmian, genuinely surprised.

'Yes, every which way,' her informant declared. 'It's not that big a dog either. A Jack Russell terrier.'

'But what about the dog?' demanded Charmian.

'I don't think it's been asked. But it's a bitch of course. It's thought he is hoping to breed a hybrid.'

'A bastard breed,' said Charmian dryly, recalling the man's appearance: short legs and a long sharp nose. 'A kind of Jackie Russell.'

On the way home, she decided against telling Humphrey either about the story or her joke. He was fond of Jack Russell dogs, had talked about having one, and might not find it funny.

Both Rewley and Dolly Barstow were back before her, sitting at their desks looking industrious which, as Charmian observed to herself, you could easily do tapping at the keys of a word processor and summoning up the internet for this information or that. Were they really waiting for her? And if so, why?

Dolly came to her room first, knocking on the door, then entering briskly.

'Inquests adjourned. No new date set. The two youngsters who found the Siddons-Jones girl said their piece. They admitted they had gone there to meet her, that she was getting them some tickets for a gig. They weren't pressed on that, although you could tell the coroner didn't believe them but had decided to go easy on them. Don't know why.' She raised an enquiring eyebrow at Charmian.

'Nothing to do with me.'

'Well, the coroner was old Lady Ferguson and she's usually pretty canny.'

'And the second inquest?'

'Even less to be learned really. The woman who found the body told her story, how she saw a foot and investigated . . . Lady Ferguson was gentle with her too. But I don't think anyone believes she did more than that. She had her dog with her and he barked so she looked to see what was worrying him. She's a tiny little creature, and the dog is the size of a cat. Hard to see either of them up for murder. I know you can't tell but . . .' Dolly shook her head. 'Frankly, anyone could get into that area at night to hide a body.'

'What about forensic evidence?'

'The Siddons girl was killed where she was found, it seems, but Felicity Harrie was not. No traces of the deed being done there. Make what you can of that.'

'The killer must know the area pretty well and also own a car or van in which to transport the body.'

'That's about it.'

Rewley pushed the door open and slid in. He was tall and slender and sliding through a half opened door was quick and easy for him.

'How about sizing up Charlie Rattle for the killings? He seems to be out and operating.'

'Not his style,' protested Dolly. She knew the Rattle family and their ways. She had dealt with Father and Mother Rattle before, their way was to grab any knife or screwdriver or chisel that came to hand, then dig it into any flesh that they happened to be near and angry with at the time.

'Style? He hasn't got style. It's a mood thing with him.'

There was some truth in this but there had never been any sex in a Rattle crime. Still, it had to start somewhere. Dolly admitted this to Rewley with a nod. 'But I still don't fancy him for it. These murders are too complicated and clever. Which he isn't.'

'Be quiet, you two, and stop batting balls across the net, this isn't a tennis match.'

'Pity we can't get Joan Dingham for it: it's got something to do with her, somehow, I swear,' said Dolly.

'Yes, I think that too,' agreed Charmian, 'and the cuts on the girls certainly suggest it, but it doesn't get us any further forward. I keep hoping that forensics will come up with something that will give us a shove but they don't.'

'So it's up to the poor bloody infantry to go plodding round the streets asking for people who might have seen or heard something.' Rewley was gloomy.

'You'd think,' said Dolly, 'that girls of that age would have gossiped a bit about where they were going and who they were meeting.' Although, she admitted silently to herself, in her day she had been a bit close mouthed about certain meetings. It all depended on how important it was.

'The one site, if I dare call it that, which they have in common was one of a series of parties, so common at university, but it was one of those crowded affairs where Jack the Ripper could have dropped in and no one would have noticed or remembered.'

'Probably he did,' said Rewley, 'or his contemporary soulmate. And we do know that the young couple who found Siddons-Jones dead had arranged to meet her there so it's possible she arranged to meet her killer there too.'

'Or he overheard the arrangement.'

'You keep saying he,' said Dolly, 'it could be she. Could be a woman.'

'Oh, you're so hot to prove that anything men can do women can do better, Dolly,' was Rewley's riposte.

'It isn't that at all.' She was indignant. 'But don't close

your eyes to possibilities. Remember Mrs West and Myra Hindley.'

'Wasn't Siddons raped?'

Charmian said crisply that there had been damage in the vaginal area but no semen had been found.

'Pity,' Rewley again. 'DNA testing would be so useful.'

'When we get to the stage of asking for that specimen from a man then we probably know who the killer is already.'

'Proof,' said Rewley succinctly.

'We need identification first.'

Dolly was gloomy. 'Could be a race against time: killers of this sort are always keen to try again.'

'I am not making out a case defending Master Charlie, whom I think is a strange little fellow, but all this is guesswork,' said Charmian. 'Nor am I against guesswork because often it comes up with the right answer, I've guessed myself, that's how detection works, but it's not enough on its own and all we have against Charlie at the moment is that we don't like him. Which is not going to get him to court.'

'You're getting sharper and sharper,' said Rewley, one of the few people who could speak to Charmian in that way. 'You need your blood sugar raising . . . Let's all go out for a pub lunch in the Duck and Whiskers in Pond Street . . . my treat, it's my birthday.'

'You had a birthday last month,' protested Dolly, but she was getting up, ready to go.

'I have one every month. Always on a Wednesday.'

Charmian got to her feet. 'I'll accept a drink but perhaps not food.'

'Dolly and I will charm you into eating one of the Duck's beef and mustard sandwiches.'

'You're very jolly today,' Charmian said suspiciously.

'Well, I used to wonder if the beef was really dead dog, but I received definite assurance from the landlord that it was dead cow. I shall have cheese and pickle myself. You can't hide much with a pickled onion.'

'You can lose friends, though.'

'Oh, Dolly, I love you, always down to earth.'

It was a wet and windy walk to the Duck, that in another day, time and age had been called the Duchess of Devonshire with a portrait of Georgiana in a big hat with a big smile.

The Duck was crowded, as it usually was at lunch-time, being near to the university and one of the big hospitals while not far from the police headquarters.

Charmian had a quick look round to see who she knew there, but slid into a corner seat without seeing a familiar face. Rewley returned with sandwiches and drinks. 'The wine isn't bad here, I got the red. Gives support and nourishment.' He turned to hand Dolly her nourishment, then stopped dead. In a low tone, he said, 'Look who's over there.' He pointed to the corner couple of seats, half hidden by curtains.

Charmian looked. 'Joan Dingham, by all that's holy.'

'Or unholy,' said Dolly. 'Who's the man?'

'I don't know.' Rewley put down his drink. 'I'm trying to get a better look.'

'Not easy.' Charmian was studying the pair. 'They've chosen a good discreet spot.'

'I wouldn't have noticed her but for the hair. No dark corner is going to quieten that down.'

The yellow cockade was not dimmed by dark spectacles and a black coat. The man with Joan Dingham was thin with his scalp shining through a closely clipped hair cut. He wore a dark suit.

Charmian was studying him, there was something about him she thought she recognized, when her mobile rang in her pocket. She turned to the wall as she spoke into it.

'Something I thought you might like to hear.' A pause while Humphrey took in a deep breath, he too may have been eating a sandwich, it sounded like it.

'Go on.'

'I took the dog for a walk.'

'That was good of you.'

'On the way, I met my old friend Dick Duckett. We used – '

'I know,' said Charmian, 'at your prep school he was known as Dickie Duckie.'

They must have had the record for the worst nick-names of any school in England.

'Yes,' Humphrey sounded mildly surprised. 'Did I tell you?'

'I'm psychic.'

'He was very pretty as a boy,' said Humphrey. 'Big success among certain circles. He's gone off a lot.'

'Spare me.'

'Did well in the war . . . well, yes. He suggested I let the dog lead the way and he might show me where he came from . . .' Another pause, while she imagined he was chewing his mouthful, she wanted to get a look at Dingham and escort.

'He led me down Darling Street and then along the main Slough road to a newish estate. Bell Road. He stopped there and just looked at me.' He waited hopefully for a word of praise for a his detective powers. 'Means something.'

'It might be very useful,' she said politely, turning back into the room for another look at Joan Dingham.

Dingham and the man had gone.

'Sorry, Humphrey, thanks for everything. I've got to go.'

Famous last words, she thought, an apology for a lot of my life, I'll probably be saying them on my deathbed.

'Where did they go?' she demanded.

Rewley was apologetic. 'A crowd of youngsters came in and when we could see through the crowd, they'd gone.'

'I think she saw us, you in particular, ma'am,' said Dolly, 'and decided to melt away.'

'She shouldn't be out on her own like that. She has only a limited freedom of movement. Where's Emily Agent? She should be with her. Or near. Ring her and find out.'

Dolly took her mobile from her pocket and went into the corner to summon Emily.

'She doesn't answer.'

'Doesn't want to,' said Charmian. 'Keep trying.'

Emily answered on the second ring. 'Sorry, sorry, I was stuck in the middle of the traffic and daren't take my hand off the wheel.'

'Oh, so you're on the road and out and about?'

'Of course I'm out and about,' said Emily crossly. 'I'm looking for that bloody woman.'

'Ah. What happened?'

'She wanted to go shopping. I took her into Caley's and she seemed to disappear into the crowd. Have you got her?'

'No, she disappeared on us too.'

'Who's us?' asked Emily. 'No, don't tell me, I can guess.'

'She's probably gone back to her sister's flat or else back to the college,' said Dolly, as she reported back to Charmian and Rewley. 'She won't want to be wandering round the city on her own.'

'She's not on her own,' Rewley pointed out.

'I'd like to know who the man is,' said Charmian. 'Joan must have wanted to see him very much.'

'Or he wanted to see her,' said Rewley, naturally seeing the man's part too.

Emily Agent caught up with Joan Dingham as she was driving down Chipper Street. She drew into the kerb and opened the door. Joan stepped in.

'You shouldn't have skipped off like that,' said Emily. 'I am supposed to stay with you. I would be in trouble if I lost you. And you might not be too happy wandering around on your own.' If indeed, you were, she thought.

'I looked around for you and couldn't find you.'

Oh, yes, thought Emily. 'The world has changed you know, the town too, since you were last in it.'

'I watched television, I know how things are.' They have changed, thought Joan, but the police are the same: watching, suspicious.

'I hope you found the friend you wanted to see,' said Emily, who had been apprised of what the other three had seen.

Joan just smiled and was mute.

'I hope you enjoyed it.' Emily let her out of the car outside her sister's flat.

Enjoyed it, thought Joan as she ran up the stairs. Enjoyed. Pleasure? And a shiver ran through her body. Right through and out the other side.

She called out to her sister, 'Lou? You there? I'm back.' There was no answer, Lou was out. She would have liked her sister's company.

She ran in to her bedroom where she threw herself on the bed.

'I am frightened,' she said aloud. 'Prison was safe. Protected.'

She had created a monster whom she could not control.

While Joan was feeling both pleasure and pain, Emily was receiving a sharp reprimand from Charmian.

'Don't let her go on the loose again. I don't want her wandering round.'

'No, I'll see to it.'

I will sit in the car all night, if need be, thought Emily, which she hoped she wouldn't have to do. She was finding this surveillance of Joan both boring and exacting. She wanted to get her hair washed.

She rang up the relief officer. 'Be ready to take over tonight.'

Baby had had a busy day, by the end of which she was tired. How life had changed, she thought, from the days when clients only wanted their hair dressed in the morning or early afternoon, but now, if it suited them, you had to stay open late as well as opening early. Even going to their houses on occasion.

Profits, of course, were good, but it was tiring.

Today's client desirous of an evening cut, wash and set, in her own home, was one of Baby's favourites. They had known each other a long while, since Evie had been a performer in a club favoured by a much younger Baby. Evie had married well, while divorcing with even more skill, and was now relatively rich. There were few secrets between them but they never dug up each other's past. Evie had a son, whom she adored, and who, as luck would have it, loved her too.

'So I'm lucky,' she said as Baby finished off her hair, 'but you've kept your looks better.'

Baby did not argue, she knew it was true. 'Well, I'm in the business. It's important how I look.' She was busy gathering up the tools of her trade, the brushes, the hand hair dryer, the mousses and the lacquers.

'My son says – ' Evie's son was a CID with the Met ' – they are all laughing and joking about Dingham's month out and saying watch who comes after her.'

'And what does that mean?'

'Oh, you know what a masochistic lot they are.'

'Macho . . .' corrected Baby absently. One of the things that friendship with Charmian had taught her was the proper use of words.

'Yes, that too. They don't believe two women could have done what they did without a man.'

'He thinks it's funny, does he?'

'Worth a laugh, he says. But you can't take too much notice of Johnnie, he's got such a sense of humour.'

Evie never offered a tip on these occasions, since Baby was such an old friend, and therefore not to be treated in this way, but when she left, a note was always pressed into Baby's hand with the murmur of 'for the staff'. This banknote Baby kept as was no doubt intended. Now she got into the car for the drive home.

The lights were on in the salon, which surprised her a little, but she had left the girls in charge and they were casual about such things.

'Don't pay the bills, that's why, the monkeys,' grumbled Baby to herself as she drove the car into her garage. She supposed Diana would be at home and she would have to give her supper and then talk to her. Although, to be fair, after her hospital session, Di was unlikely to want to talk.

She tried the door to the salon. Not locked. Really she would have to talk to the staff. 'The door must be locked when you leave,' she would say.

She walked in quickly and deposited the bag with her professional tools in it, before looking around. The salon was tidy enough, couldn't fault the girls there.

She could see a head, Diana's head over the top of the big chair. As she looked, Di's hand hung loosely over the arm.

'Oh, Di,' she called out, 'you've done this once to me already. Lay off. A joke is a joke, but not twice.'

She walked round to confront Diana, and as she did so, Diana slid sideways in the chair. Her scarf had been tightly drawn round her neck. And this time there was no joke. Diana was dead.

Baby immediately called Charmian. 'I thought you'd be the best person to call . . . you'd tell me what to do.'

'You must call the uniformed branch, they will handle it.'

'I knew you'd tell me what to do.'

Charmian nodded; she suspected that Baby knew anyway but wanted help. Someone to stand beside her.

'And you were elected,' Charmian told herself sardonically.

'The police surgeon will come to certify that Diana is dead.'

'Oh, she's dead all right.'

'Then she'll be taken away.'

'To the police mortuary?'

'They usually use the one in the University Hospital.'

'Oh, good, that's a nice one. Oh, poor Di, she valued the comforts of life so much. They'll look after her, won't they?'

'You can be sure of that. You can arrange the funeral in due course if you want to.'

'I wonder who will come.' Baby was staring down at her friend's dead body.

'She has friends and family, I expect.'

'No family.' She hesitated. 'All right, I'll do what I can: I'll phone now. I'd like to tidy her up, but I suppose I mustn't?'

'Leave her the way she is.' Charmian added carefully, 'After all, someone did kill her, she didn't do this herself and there will be an investigation.'

'I do understand. It's been a shock though.'

'Of course it has,' said Charmian with sympathy.

'You're used to bodies.'

Charmian opened her mouth in protest, then shut it again. Not worth a comment. How could she say: however often you see bodies you never get used to them.

'Look, I'm coming over.'

Baby seemed to have no fear for herself although death had come so close to her. You could call it courage or lack of imagination. Probably a mixture of both. She went to the telephone to make her call to the police, doing it calmly and efficiently. Then she felt dizzy. 'I'm fainting,' she thought, 'I never faint.' But blackness came down.

When she came to, Charmian was sitting in one of the big chairs in the salon, offering her a glass of water. Baby brushed it away irritably.

'Of course, like I said: you're used to it.'

'You never get used to it.'

Baby accepted this, while not quite believing it. 'But thanks for coming. Sorry if I am behaving badly. I can't quite imagine Di letting herself be killed, but she could be very arrogant. And what with one thing and another, I don't know how much she minded dying . . . it was going to happen anyway.'

'I expect she minded. I would. One likes a bit of free will.'

Baby nodded.

'Do you know why anyone should want to kill her?

Baby shook her head. 'Not to say "know" but she didn't like Joan and her sister and I don't think they liked her. Or trusted her. Joan used to make odd remarks and jokes about Diana. But Joan couldn't have killed her, she's watched all the time.'

Charmian agreed. She had already felt the presence of a third person walking the stage. Unluckily, she could put neither a face nor a name to this person.

'Any ideas?' she asked Baby. Baby had a knack of picking up information, although this did not mean that she would pass it on.

If Baby knew anything now, then she was not saying. She shook her head. 'All I can think about now is Di. I don't know who did it, or why or how. The only thing

I do know is that it must be connected with Joan somehow. Or the latest murders . . . Might be the same thing, they look like a present for Joan, with her badge on them.'

Baby could be very perceptive sometimes, which made you realize how clever she really was and that the breathless, feathery appearance was really a facade. She had after all built up a successful business and here she was still running it. This made her unique among her former sisters in crime.

Charmian stayed with her until the local CID unit arrived and then, aware that Baby would be well looked after by them and also that Charmian's own presence would not be welcome, she took herself off.

She stood outside for a moment trying to think things through: she was surprised to find that she grieved for Diana, but she did. The woman had the right to those last weeks of life (which being Diana she might somehow have stretched out for longer), and she didn't deserve to die that way but comfortably in bed. Charmian felt outraged on Diana's behalf. She remembered the time they had both had tests in a hospital clinic and she had come through healthy while Diana had been told she had the seeds of the illness that eventually would otherwise have killed her.

'Would have done,' thought Charmian. 'But it wasn't given time.

She drove home to pour out to her husband the latest drama. 'I am quite sure it is all part of the same story: Joan coming home and the murder of the two girls.'

Her husband looked at her sceptically. 'Are you sure this is not just your dramatic imagination?'

'It's happened, may happen again.'

'Heaven forbid.'

'There is a connection, quite clear in this case: she was threatening Joan.'

'Are you accusing Joan? Or her sister? Or her son?'

Charmian had to admit she did not know. She was flailing round wanting to accuse somebody but not sure whom.

'Have a drink and calm down,' advised her prudent husband. But she was not to be at peace for long.

The phone rang just as he was pouring them both some wine.

'Dolly speaking . . . I am down here at Baby's, they want us here. Can you come?'

Chapter Nine

'Sex comes into it somewhere, doesn't it?' said Dolly, as she stood with Charmian looking down at Diana's body. 'With these killings, I mean. It has to.'

Charmian turned aside. The room was crowded with the police team. The police surgeon had just withdrawn after pronouncing Diana dead.

'Strangled.'

'How long?' Charmian had asked.

He had consulted his thermometer. 'Still warm, not long, two hours at the most, perhaps less.'

The forensic team was already at work while SOCO concentrated on seeing that everything at the crime scene got the attention it deserved. A photographer was working with her. The Scene of Crime Officer was a woman, the newly promoted Sergeant Beth Dyer.

It was as the photographer got into position for yet another shot that Dolly had made her pronouncement.

'Sex came into everything with Diana,' said Charmian, sadly.

'That isn't quite what I meant . . . It's just a feeling, an intuition. Somehow, I find myself connecting this death here with the murders of the first girls. With Joan Dingham.'

'Joan certainly had no love for Diana. But Emily Agent will have been keeping an eye on her.'

'She wasn't doing so well this morning.'

'No, but I rang up and gave her a rocket. She promised not to let Joan out of her sight. She's got a substitute to stand in for her when necessary.'

'It's the man,' worried Dolly. 'What about the man we saw with Joan in the pub?'

'Got to find out who he is first, and that means talking to Joan.'

By this time, Diana's body was being prepared to go off to the mortuary where the pathologist would examine it to make certain of the cause of death.

'I will talk to Joan myself,' said Charmian, 'but first I must speak to Baby again. Not something I am looking forward to.'

Baby was sitting in a large chair before a low table on which was a bottle of whisky. She faced Charmian with tears in her eyes. She was crying neatly and quietly, not disturbing her make-up, but every so often a large round tear would roll down her cheek. 'Oh, you again.'

'I came back to see how you were.'

'Lousy. Rotten. I feel guilty; I let her down.'

'That is not true.' Charmian sat down beside Baby. 'Come on. Beryl Andrea Barker, stop crying and act your age. Diana's death is not your fault. She was murdered, killed by someone who wanted her killed and whom you could not stop.'

'But here, in my salon . . .'

'Here or anywhere, if that killer wanted her, then

he would get her. That's how it works, take my word for it. A really determined killer always gets through.'

Baby sat up and dabbed her eyes. 'You're right, of course. And what I must do now is help you find who killed her.' She frowned. 'You said he, but supposing the killer is a woman?'

'Who do you have in mind? Better say.' Because I think I know what you are going to say. Name the name.

'Joan Dingham.'

'I knew you were going to say Joan.'

'She hated Diana, she'd be glad to have her dead. And she knows how to kill.'

Charmian shook her head. 'No opportunity . . . She's watched. She can't just slip out and kill.' Even as she said it, she remembered that Joan had done just that earlier that day. 'I will be talking to her, of course, and having her movements checked.' I thought of her myself, she might have said, of course I did, but I can't see how she could have done it.

Why, yes, the book Lou and Pip were bleating about, and the power to do it. She knows she can kill. But how would she have the opportunity? Charmian asked herself again.

'It's not clear whether Diana struggled,' she said aloud, 'but the pathologist will let us know.'

'Diana would struggle,' said Baby with conviction. 'Yes, she sure would struggle.'

'We will find out. There will be traces. With luck the killer will have left something for the forensic boys.'

'She would struggle,' repeated Baby, as if she had not said this already. 'But she was ill, very ill. The cancer had come back. I don't know how much strength there was in her. She was dying.'

Both women were silent for a moment.

'Rotten luck,' said Charmian.

'Not even allowed to die in her own time.' Baby kicked the table leg in front of her. 'Bugger, bugger.' She rubbed her foot. 'I didn't even like her much. She landed on me here, unasked. I didn't turn her away, although I guess I might have done if it had gone on longer. But I thought she was dying.' She started to walk up and down the room. 'She didn't deserve to die like that.'

Charmian nodded to indicate that she felt the same and understood. 'Not your fault,' she said. 'You were good to her, that's what counts.'

'But I feel guilty.'

'If it's any comfort to you, I feel the same.'

'Thanks, I don't know that it does help, but I'm glad you said it.'

'I'll be off,' said Charmian. 'Will you be all right here? You won't exactly be alone, police teams of one sort or another will be here all night.' Apologetically, she said, 'You won't be able to open tomorrow, I'm afraid.'

Baby gave a shudder. 'No. I'm not sure if I will ever want to open the salon again.'

'Would you like to come and stay with me?'

Baby smiled at her. 'Thanks for the offer, but no. I'll stay here, it is my home, I have to get used to the idea of living here and, as you say, I will have a police guard.'

'You will have to come down to the office to make a statement tomorrow. I'm not sure who will be in charge, probably not me.'

'I hope it is you. There might be things I want to say about Diana and her life that I may not want to tell anyone else.'

'Anything you can think of at the moment?'

'No.' Baby shook her head. 'Lou was going on this morning about how Joan hated Di. I don't think Lou liked her all that much either.'

'Don't pass judgement on anyone too soon. That's my advice.'

Baby nodded. 'Rotten friends I've got.'

Charmian patted her arm with sympathy. 'You're in shock.' She went to the door. 'I'm there if you want me. Or,' she added hopefully, 'if you think of anything that might help.'

'What sort of thing?'

'Oh, it depends. Someone hanging around the salon whom you wouldn't expect to see or don't recognize, anything out of the ordinary, really.'

Baby said slowly that she couldn't think of anything. She accompanied Charmian to the door, walking down the stairs with her. She stopped short just before they got to ground level where the salon was.

A uniformed man stood outside the door on the pavement where several police cars lined the kerb. A small crowd had gathered.

'Is that a TV van?'

Charmian looked. She nodded. 'Yes.'

'Di would have been pleased. Pity she doesn't know.'

'Maybe she does.' Her friends the white witches would have assured her that Diana was still around and watching. Pity she can't drop in and tell us who did it, thought Charmian.

Baby stood looking, she felt no desire to get herself on the TV screen, which was amazing really, because there had been a time when she would have killed for it.

She started to go back up to what she now felt was

the secure cave of her own set of rooms where she could crawl away and hide.

A picture came into her mind.

'Charmian,' she said. 'There is something: this evening, before I went off to do Evie's hair, there was a dog hanging about the front.'

Charmian went away, meditating on what Baby had said about the dog. Which dog? Before she could give her mind intelligently to the question of the dog, she was caught by an anxious telephone call from Emily Agent.

'Can you come up here? To the flat. Joan has attacked her sister. Broken her nose, I think, we've got the doctor coming. I think you ought to speak to Joan before the doctor sedates her.'

'On my way. I was coming anyway. You know what's happened down here?'

'Of course.'

'Is that what it's about?'

Charmian could almost feel Emily shrug across the telephone line. She was silent for a space.

Charmian drove over fast, parked the car then ran up the stairs. Emily met her on the last few steps.

'She wants you,' said Emily. 'It's my fault, she heard me talking on my mobile about what had happened to Diana.'

'Who? Joan Dingham?'

'Yes, she flew into a rage. She's gone mute again. Or trying to. She's trying to hide inside silence.'

'That's perceptive of you.'

'Speech might burst out of her at any moment. There's a big conversation going on inside her, you can almost hear it. God knows what words she'll put to it when it does get out. But Lou wants you too. She's talking, poor soul, as far as she can through a bloody nose.'

She was leading Charmian up the stairs and into the flat as she spoke.

'Doctor here yet?'

'Any minute.' She paused in the hall where the jug of flowers on the bow-fronted table still celebrated Joan's return. She nodded towards the sitting room. 'They're in there . . .'

'Was it safe to leave them?'

'Yes, Pip's there. Lou phoned him and he came running over.' Emily added thoughtfully. 'In a funny kind of way they are all close. But who loves who and who hates who I can't make out.'

The sitting-room door opened, Pip put his head round it. 'Thought it might be the doctor.'

'On his way.'

'Aunt Lou's nose could do with help. Bleeding like a pig. Mum shouldn't have whacked her.'

Joan was sitting silently on the sofa in the window while Lou sat on an upright chair by a table. Charmian recalled that the drinks had been on that table at the party. Lou was holding a towel, which was indeed blood-stained but not as badly as Charmian had feared, to her nose, she had known noses that bled more freely. The room was quiet with Joan not talking and Lou also silent. Perhaps mutism was a family habit. And, come to think of it, if you were a family with the deadly secrets this lot might have had, then speechlessness might not be a bad habit to have.

Then Lou stood up and, trailing the bloody towel,

came towards Charmian, hand held out, Lady Macbeth style.

'I'm sorry but my sister has made a serious accusation against me and I thought you ought to hear it. Sergeant Agent thought so too.' She looked at Emily, who nodded. 'She thinks I killed Diana.'

'You did,' suddenly Joan had found her voice.

'Oh come on, Mum,' said Pip. 'You know she couldn't have done. Why should she?'

'She strangled Diana. It has to have been her. I don't know why. There doesn't have to be a why.'

And there speaks the authentic voice of experience, thought Charmian.

'I think we can soon establish when Diana was killed, and if you can show you were nowhere near the salon at that time, then you don't have to worry.'

'I went to my office first, then I was out walking in the afternoon,' said Lou. 'I like to take a long walk.'

'Someone will have seen you, I expect,' said Charmian patiently. 'And there is always forensic evidence. If you killed Diana, you will have left traces in the salon.'

'Of course, I left traces there,' said Lou, through the muffling towel. 'I had my hair done there today, didn't I? And I went back later on to leave a tip for the girl who prepares the shampoos and tints. I always do, but I had forgotten.'

Charmian frowned. Not likely that Lou was the killer, but not impossible either, she began to think.

'If anyone saw you and comes forward we will know,' she said. 'Or perhaps you will recall something.' To Joan, she said, 'Who was the man with you in the pub at lunchtime today?'

'What? What's this?' asked Lou sharply. 'What have you been doing?'

Joan did not answer.

'By God, I ought to have hit *your* nose,' said Lou.

Charmian intervened. 'I wish you could suggest someone who saw you on your walk.'

Wearily, Lou said, 'Only Baby's dog, if that counts. He could give me a bark, I daresay, if he would. I think I saw him in the park. On his own.'

'Baby doesn't have a dog.'

Lou shrugged. 'I thought I saw him hanging about her place once or twice.'

Charmian moved across to look at Joan directly, Joan moved her eyes away.

'Joan, what did the cruciform symbol mean that was carved on the skin of the girls you killed? It meant something.'

Joan's face did not change. She went on staring into space.

'You don't remember? No? Well, you'd better start remembering, dig something out of your memory because otherwise I'll make it my business to see you go back inside for a long time.' It was not an idle threat, she could probably do it. 'You can forget the degree course, you'll go back immediately.'

She turned to Lou. 'Likewise you, Lou. Get together the two of you and tell me a story I can believe.'

She knew she was angry, probably making things worse, and certainly making threats to Joan that were unwise.

The door bell rang as Charmian was trying to sort herself out. Emily said, 'The doctor. At last.'

It was Dr Farmer, who did a lot of police work, who

came in with Inspector Parker. Parker gave Emily the sort of look that blamed her for what had happened.

Charmian got herself away as soon as she could. 'I don't suppose Lou wants to make a charge against her sister, but get them both to make statements, if you can. I'll see them both in the morning.'

As she walked out, her eye subliminally took in a photograph on the wall, a group photograph. Something to look at some time, she registered, when she wasn't in such a hurry.

'Pity she didn't get the dog's autograph,' said Dolly somewhat sourly. 'Or a photograph.'

Back at SRADIC, Charmian had produced the story of Joan's attack on her sister, her accusation and Lou's attempt at an alibi.

'Plenty of dogs on the loose in this town,' observed Rewley, who was sitting on the edge of Charmian's desk as she telephoned her husband.

'Get off,' she said, giving the desk a push to dislodge him. 'Humphrey? Where's the dog?'

'Haven't seen it all day. On the loose. Took off after we came home from the park. I expect it'll be back soon. Knows where the food is, smart fellow. Why?'

'That dog comes into it somewhere,' said Charmian savagely. 'Puts his nose in everywhere.' She put the phone down. 'But I don't believe Lou killed Diana, I'd be surprised if Joan really thinks so. It's a puzzle why she attacked her sister.'

'Just a domestic,' drawled Rewley, 'Lou's always been the man in that family so when there's trouble, she gets it in the neck.'

'You don't mean?' Dolly said heatedly.

'No, Lou's not lesbian, or if she is, not active,' said Charmian, who had been reading the records of the Dingham murders twenty years before. 'It was thought that the Rhos-Joan relationship had that element, probably did, but nothing was established.'

It was late and they were all tired, but no one was getting home just yet.

Charmian started to walk round the room. 'We've picked up the police gossip of the time which was that there was a third person involved in those earlier killings and that that person was a man. Today, we saw Joan having a drink with a man.'

'Bald head, that's all we know,' said Rewley. 'Wish we'd nabbed him on the spot.'

'The dog,' said Charmian, 'came from Dr Harrie.'

'So?'

'I called in a favour or two and an old colleague is checking something for me. I am waiting for a call back.'

'I daresay I could tell you now,' said Rewley, who had been showing his own signs of impatience.

'I expect so. But let's wait to get it authenticated, shall we?'

The telephone rang, Charmian reached out for it quickly. But it was her husband.

'You must have been sitting right by the phone. One ring.'

'I was.'

'The dog is back.'

'Has he got blood on his paws?'

'What do you mean? Has he been in an accident? He looks fine.'

'No, only joking, but he seems to be the alibi for a suspect accused of killing Diana . . .'

'Really?' Humphrey sounded sceptical. 'How did he manage that?'

'He seems to have been sighted outside Baby's place and then in the Great Park where the suspect was walking.'

'He is tired, and there are certainly some leaves and mud on his coat. I thought he might have been looking for Dr Harrie. Any news there?'

'Not yet.'

'You need a bit of luck,' said Humphrey knowledgeably. 'When a chap is missing, it takes time and luck to track him down . . . And then a doctor, if he wanted to do himself in, could tuck himself away somewhere and just put himself to sleep. He might even go home to do it. He did have a home, I suppose?'

'Oh, yes. Birdie thinks it was in London so the Met are doing the looking.'

He was probably still alive, wandering round, wondering what to do. He hadn't seemed the suicidal type, but you could never tell.

'Good, good. Now don't you worry, he'll turn up. Somewhere.' Humphrey assured her.

'I might be late back. Don't wait up for me.'

'Shall I come down? Bring you some sandwiches and coffee?'

Looking at her tired colleagues, Charmian said that wasn't a bad idea. 'Bring enough for three.'

'Will do.'

'Humphrey is bringing us food and coffee,' she announced.

Rewley admitted he was hungry. 'I was thinking of

going to the all-night deli in Apron Street. They make good sandwiches.'

Charmian was about to start on a defence of her husband's sandwiches when there was a smart, double rap on her door. 'Must be the night man,' she said, referring to the officer who remained on duty in SRADIC all night. She went to the door.

Outside stood the night man and behind him the uniformed figure of Sergeant Tiller from the Slough Division.

'A body of a man has been dragged from the river above Wraysbury. Seems to fit the description of Dr Harrie.' Tiller hesitated, perhaps surprised to see the trio. 'I was told I would find you here. I have the car outside.'

Charmian knew she must go. She had asked to be told at once of any likely suicide victims and here one was. Pull a string or two, she thought, and you find it is you that is on the end of it. Plus a body or two. Dr Harrie had to be considered because of his granddaughter. He had had an interest other than pure curiosity.

And now Diana, who had planned to profit from writing a book about the first murders and Joan Dingham, had been killed.

It's like a piece of knitting, except I don't think I have the pattern right, Charmian thought to herself.

'I'll come.' she turned to the other two. 'Tell Humphrey I will be back, and to keep the coffee hot.'

'Shall I come with you?' asked Dolly.

Charmian shook her head. 'No, I'll be fine.' The drowned man, whoever he was, could not have been in the river for long, so he could not yet be blown out of shape or discoloured.

'Where is he?'

'Slough mortuary, ma'am. He was pulled out of the river this afternoon but it all took time.'

She nodded. She would have preferred to have been summoned to the riverside earlier rather than the mortuary at night, but that was not how things were done.

If it is indeed you lying on the mortuary slab, Dr Harrie, I must take back some of the suspicious thoughts I have been having about you.

The sergeant was silent as he settled her in the car, then took his own seat beside the driver. She was a pretty young woman who gave Charmian a big smile. Nice haircut and good teeth. She looked good in uniform, too.

I looked good in uniform, Charmian recalled, in my day. Not difficult, you just needed a trim waist and long legs. Maybe that's why I joined the Force. I had a good degree, could have done anything with it, and the police wasn't exactly fashionable at the time. Is it ever?

As Charmian was driven away, the telephone on her desk rang. Rewley looked at Dolly, who nodded, then picked it up.

Charmian was back within the hour. Her husband, plus dog, had arrived before her. He had set out a plate of sandwiches and a big Thermos of coffee on her desk which he was sitting studying with interest. The dog was at his feet, sound asleep: work for the day was over.

They all stood up when Charmian came in except the dog, who slept on. No one spoke until she said quickly, 'No, not the right man. This poor fellow was younger and thinner and I had never seen his face before. Not Dr Harrie.'

'No,' said Rewley. 'Not Dr Harrie. In fact, it couldn't be. We've just discovered there is no Dr Harrie. Not alive, anyway, he died some years ago, Felicity had no grandfather.'

'Well, well,' said Charmian. 'Why is that no surprise to me?'

Humphrey poured out mugs of coffee (he had brought some with him) and unwrapped the sandwiches. Quietly, he passed the plate round. The dog woke up and followed him.

No one else was greatly surprised either.

On the way home, with Humphrey driving, his basket of provender now eaten, he said, 'He always was a doubtful fellow, I didn't know what to make of him. You don't, do you, with a chap who looks like that?'

'You gave him a touch of respectability when you pretended to remember him from school.'

'Prep school,' Humphrey said at once. 'Little boys, long while ago. People change. I've changed.'

Yes, thought Charmian, thinking of what Humphrey must have been like at this early school: long legged, always tall for his age, a crest of unbrushed fair hair (he still had plenty of hair, thank goodness), full of talk and information, most of it accurate. She hadn't known him then, but she could imagine, and perhaps he hadn't changed all that much.

'I hope you find him soon,' he said.

Over breakfast the next morning, Humphrey said, 'I think you owe it to Birdie and Winifred to tell them yourself. This morning.' He went back to eating his boiled egg, and reading *The Times*, duty done.

Charmian ate a piece of toast, and gave some to the dog. Then she urged her husband to take his face out of the newspaper so she could talk to him.

'Now stop acting the Wisest Old Man in the village, it's a good part, and you've written it well.' Humphrey kept a straight face. 'And tell me what you really think about the missing so-called Dr Harrie.'

'He was certainly not a doctor. A man with a personality problem and probably deeply unhappy.'

'And would he kill himself?'

'It's your job to know that, isn't it?'

'Have a go. I need an outside opinion.'

Her husband considered, then he said, 'Yes, one way and another, I believe he would.'

Charmian nodded. 'Right.'

'He treated the dog well, though.'

'But I told you, more or less, I told you,' said Birdie, when Charmian called to alert them to the latest news. 'It was all that hair, I said that our visitor had that to hide behind. I could tell he was hiding. Mind,' she added thoughtfully, 'there are more things than who you are that you might have to hide.'

'He *was* hiding.' Charmian felt she had to say this.

'Of course, but what was he hiding from and why, I ask myself? What did he talk about a lot? Himself and the death of his granddaughter. But he knew she was not his granddaughter, so he was talking about himself and death.'

Birdie had a knack of saying profound things so simply and artlessly that it took time to sink in.

'There is a search going on for him,' said Charmian.

'Of course. But no one knows now who he is: he has no name.'

'Do you think he is dead, Birdie? Was the threat of suicide real?'

Birdie looked thoughtful. 'My dear, with men of that sort one can never be sure. What was he doing here? What did that charade mean to him? And Charmian . . . since he knew he could camp at the end of our garden and not be turned away. I think he knew of us, the two white witches of Windsor.'

'I thought that too,' said Charmian.

'His real home may not be too far away.'

'I thought the same. I was hoping the dog would lead the way, but so far, he hasn't.'

'Do you think he is dead?'

Birdie paused to think. 'Can't say. Sorry. But I do think he is a deeply disturbed person who is very interested in murders.'

Winifred came into the room, carrying a bowl of purple and pink flowers. 'The hellebore is doing very well this year, Birdie, so I ventured to pick some. Although I always think it very funereal, don't you?'

'Never seen any in a wreath,' said Birdie.

'Oh, no, they are a private flower, not a ceremonial one. A private flower for private mourning.' She planted the flowers on the table. 'You are talking about the hoaxer? Hoaxer Harrie,' she said with some pleasure.

'You knew what he was or wasn't?' asked Charmian. Her friends often amazed her.

'We knew he was a bit iffy, didn't we. Birdie? But we

like that rather than otherwise. He was an attractive man,' she said appreciatively.

'Birdie thinks he was too absorbed with death.'

Winifred shrugged. 'Birdie likes a bit of drama.'

'Now now,' protested Birdie. 'But he could do with finding. We know about the death in the hairdressers. Word gets around quickly here. And being witches we have special channels.'

I bet, thought Charmian.

'I didn't know Diana, and we do our own hair, don't we, Winifred, but it's a terrible thing to happen. Is there a suspect?'

Birdie had a lovely formal way of putting things, Charmian thought, she would never say: have you caught anyone yet?

Cautiously, Charmian admitted that an accusation had been made against someone, but she did not think that person was guilty.

Birdie frowned. 'A woman, I suppose.'

'Why do you say that?'

'My thoughts tell me that no man killed Diana.'

Charmian went back home and then drove to her office, leaving her husband and the dog with instructions to go out for a walk together to see if the dog could flush out his former master.

In the office there was a fax telling her that Joan Dingham had now withdrawn her accusation against her sister and had apologized for the attack on her. She said it was just 'nerves'. The fax was from Inspector Parker who managed, even in writing, to sound sceptical and disapproving of Joan Dingham.

Dolly came in. 'You got the fax?'

'You've seen it?'

'No, but Emily Agent rang to tell me about it. She would like to strangle Joan herself.'

'No other news? Nothing that takes us forward?'

Dolly said, 'No. No progress. Well, nothing that anyone is saying anything about. Of course, they might be keeping a fact or two up their sleeves, but I doubt it.'

'Three murders,' said Charmian. 'The death toll is rising.' She flipped through the copy of the report that the CID investigating team had sent.

Witnesses interviewed. Not many of them and none with anything interesting to say.

Forensic reports: mud on the Siddons girl, dried sand on the Harrie girl . . . nothing surprising in either cases since they were traces of the ground where their bodies had rested. Scraps of leaves and grass. All local, nothing illuminating. The injuries on both girls had been done with a pointed, sharp knife. The injuries on the last victim had, at first, seemed like a savage rape but which, it was later confirmed, was not. She had been dead when so injured.

The killer was getting inventive but, in a funny kind of way, kinder. The girl had known nothing of the last set of injuries.

Charmian turned to her diary. 'What's going on today?'

'Yes, I know,' Dolly was following her gaze. 'Today, this morning in fact, the parents of the two murdered girls, the Pinckney Heath girl and the Windsor one, are holding a joint press interview. TV as well, I believe.'

Charmian was running through the names. 'I hate these occasions but I suppose I had better go. John

Parker made a point of asking me. Mrs Goodison, that's the Harrie girl's mother, who has come back from Canada, and the Siddons girl's parents, they wish to be called that so it seems, have come back from South Africa. I suppose any publicity is better than none.'

'That's a bit sour, isn't it?'

'Oh, I'll be there, might get a clue about the so-called Dr Harrie.'

'I'd like to come,' said Dolly tentatively.

'There's plenty for you to get on with here. Rewley too.' Charmian looked around. 'Where is he, by the way?'

'Went off to Kingston to look at some hospital records. Didn't say why.'

'He should have done. I'm running this ship. Right, you can come with me, in that case. I'll meet you in an hour and you can drive me to the St Anselm church hall where the press conference is being held.'

Still sour, thought Dolly as she went away. Not like her. No, wrong to call her sour: she blames herself for getting no further with this case. She doesn't understand Joan Dingham either and that isn't helping. But who does understand that woman?

The room where the parents and the police were facing press and television reporters was crowded. The police had organized the session. Charmian, surveying the faces, thought she recognized one or two but could not put names to them.

Joan Dingham was not there, which was wise, nor was her sister Lou, presumably still sporting her black eye and broken nose, on whom the latest word was that the nose was not broken, but badly bruised. But another face that Charmian associated with the Dinghams, the helpful man in the garden around the flat where Lou lived – Chappell, was that his name? – he was there, looking keenly interested. He'll probably report back to Joan and Lou, speculated Charmian, he looks the eager sort that longs to tell you something. Very often something you don't want to know.

Charmian took a seat at the back of the room where Dolly had joined her. 'Be good to have a smoke,' said Dolly.

'No, it wouldn't. You should give it up.' Charmian was sharp.

'You used to smoke.'

'And now I don't.'

'The truth is, I don't enjoy these sessions.'

'Neither do I,' admitted Charmian.

'It's the tears,' said Dolly sadly, 'and then those who try to hide the tears. Cover them up.'

'This lot look calm enough.'

Mrs Goodison, beautifully dressed in a dark suit, with a flame-coloured scarf at her throat, was sitting very upright, the tension only showing by the tight grip she had on her handbag. She herself was not beautiful but very attractive, even considering the stiffness of her iron composure.

She's not going to cry, Charmian thought, but she might surprise us all by standing up and shouting. Wouldn't blame her, either.

Mr and Mrs Siddons were both wearing black: black and white striped and floating silk for her, and a short black jacket with jeans for him. They sat a few feet away from each other with a policewoman in between.

'He's wearing Armani,' whispered Dolly. 'Last season's though.'

The Siddonses were treating the press conference as a public performance and, although Charmian thought they would not burst into tears or shout but behave with appropriate dignity, she guessed they would go away afterwards and have a strong gin and tonic.

Mrs Siddons had her hair dressed in several small plaits, which was oddly becoming to her face.

'She could pick a fight, that one,' whispered Dolly.

'She's an actress, you can tell,' was all Charmian said, although she thought Dolly was right.

The parents, all three of them, were introduced by Inspector Patrick Palmer, who was the new man in charge of public relations and was known as Publicity Pat. He did his usual job and first Mrs Goodison and then both the Siddonses spoke a few words, telling of their distress and shock and urging anyone who might know anything to come forward.

The television camera took them all in, they made a handsome and interesting set of parents. A cut above the usual parents of murder victims, and more in control of themselves. They had dressed for the occasion as if it was a wedding.

Charmian felt sure that they were loving parents but not one of them had been in the country at the time of the killings: the Harrie child, Felicity, had been living as a boarder in a school house while the Siddons girl had looked after herself. Both girls had enjoyed the freedom and had moved into racier society than they might have managed otherwise.

Perhaps this was why they had died.

Charmian met Mrs Goodison's eyes at this point but

realized that they were not focused on her, she was not looking at anything in the crowded room, she was staring into space. Then she stood up, throwing her handbag to the floor, and began to shout.

The television camera concentrated on her.

'None of you are interested in my dead child, you are not going to find out who killed her, you just came to see a show.'

The television cameras continued to stay on her face, but Charmian knew that nothing of this would be shown on the screen, but would be edited out.

She's going to say something really awkward any minute now, Charmian thought.

'You let that bloody murderer Dingham out of prison and now look what's happened. It's her, all her. Kill her, kill her.'

That would be edited out too, Charmian thought.

Chapter Ten

'I knew she was going to blow up with something, I could see it coming,' Charmian said as they walked away. 'Of course, it's rubbish what she said but I can't help feeling there is something in it.'

Outside in the road, there was a rough-haired figure pacing up and down.

'That dog,' said Charmian, 'what is he doing here?'

'Came to find you, I expect,' said Dolly, but without believing it. She had never seen an animal so set on pursuing its own agenda as this mongrel, and she did not think Charmian was on it.

'I'll take the dog back and shut him up.'

But the dog, faithful to his own plans, had disappeared.

There followed one of those periods of calm when nothing much seemed to be happening in any of the cases that interested Charmian and her team.

Rewley seemed to find what he was doing in Kingston interesting but he was reserved about what, if anything, he got from it. He was still working on it: Archival work was always slow, he explained, but he did not neglect any of the other cases he was working on, and produced his usual meticulous reports on time. He was also preoccupied with looking for Charlie Rattle, who remained elusive. He rejected all ideas that Charlie might have skipped the country on the grounds that no country in the world would accept Charlie on his appearance alone, not to mention that he had no money and no passport. 'He's around,' Rewley claimed, 'this is the only world he knows. Only I haven't found him yet.'

Dolly was preoccupied with a possible child-abuse case in a family hostel. Her energies were, for the moment, diverted from the local murders.

All of them in SRADIC were used to working on more than one problem at once. They were expected, as Charmian said once, to be as many headed as a hydra.

Beryl Andrea Barker's hairdressing salon in Windsor was still closed by the police while they went over it, even including Baby's private apartments.

'They suspect me,' said Baby on the telephone to Charmian. 'I know they do. Can't blame 'em.'

Charmian had demurred but she knew it was true. Baby was a suspect, more for want of anyone else.

'I'm moving my stylists and assistants to the Slough establishment, it's not far away, and I shall give a reduction to clients who follow me there. For the first few appointments, anyway,' added Baby frugally. 'And as soon as I get the police off the Windsor place, I'll ask my old friend, Mr Chappell, to come and remodel the whole salon so there is no memory left of what happened there. I will wipe it all out.' With her usual hard-headed good sense, she said, 'It needed doing anyway. You'll follow me, won't you?'

Charmian was reassuring. 'Of course. I won't abandon you.'

'I thought you'd say that. And I think most of my clients will follow me.' She added, a touch smugly, 'I do Lady Brittlebay's hair now, you know, she writes the best detective stories anyone ever wrote. Enormous sales.' Baby respected that part, no need to read the books, just to know that much. 'I've made a great improvement to her hair.'

'I thought you'd cut most of it off.'

'Well, you have to be ruthless. And a short cut eliminates a lot of problems.'

Charmian ran her hand over her hair and resolved not to be barbered into oblivion.

'She cried a bit at first, well, that's natural, happens to quite a few ladies. But you have to talk them through it, I said, "Get yourself some lovely big earrings. Gold and a bit of glitter . . . and some dark spectacles and you'll be surprised how you look."'

'I understand she was,' said Charmian.

Later that day, Charmian went to call on Joan Dingham. Before this visit, she spoke to Dr Greenham about her.

'How's she doing?'

'We've had quite a few upsets, haven't we?' he replied cautiously. 'The odd murder. But she seems over that now. She's a hard worker, reads all the books, takes notes at the lectures. She's in the library a lot. Written work is a bit weak but we can help with that. Yes, she's got the potential for a good student.'

'I thought I'd go to see her again. The last time we met she was a bit up in the clouds . . .' She paused.

'Yes, she accused the sister of killing that woman Diana.'

'Rubbish, of course. No one believed it.'

'I was willing to,' said Dr Greenham. 'In fact, I think I would have been pleased if she had . . .' he paused ' . . . I don't like either of them, you know.'

'Not even the sister?'

'No, there's something about them that worries me. Call me imaginative, if you like.'

I might call you prejudiced, said Charmian to herself.

'When is the best time to go visiting?'

'Joan has a lecture and a tutorial this morning.'

'Right.'

So that's when I will go, she thought, I'll see Lou on her own. Also do some looking round. I will telephone ahead to make sure she is in.

She drove round to Lou's in her own car. 'Make it informal,' she told herself. 'Keep it casual.'

Emily was not there, she was at the lecture with Joan, but Lou was at home. She was welcoming.

'Glad to see you, Miss Daniels. Come in. You want to see Joan, I expect? She's at a lecture.'

Charmian avoided a direct answer. 'She's doing well, isn't she?'

'Very well, so they say. And she's happy doing it. She's always been clever.'

'Yes,' agreed Charmian. She had never thought Joan stupid.

'Like a drink? Coffee, sherry?'

'Coffee would be fine, thank you.'

'You sit there by the window while I get some. I would enjoy a cup myself.'

While Lou disappeared into the kitchen, Charmian looked around her.

A neat, well-furnished room with a sofa and matching chairs covered in flowered chintz, the curtains were a different material but the colour harmonized. Pale carpet covered the floor. A few books on the table, they looked like books which Joan was using. One big picture on the wall, a reproduction of a Constable landscape.

And there was the photograph which had interested her: a row of girls in school uniform. She thought she could recognize Joan. On the breast of each girl was a badge, the design of which closely resembled the carving cut into the flesh of Joan's victims and again, although less skilfully, on the two recent murdered girls.

The photograph was simply pasted onto a pale green card. Charmian would have picked it up for a closer look but Lou returned with the coffee.

'That's a school photograph of Joan,' said Lou. 'I kept it by me because for years it was the only photograph I had of her. I keep it out now for old times' sake, I suppose.'

'You must have missed her.'

'It was more complicated than that,' said Lou with a slight smile. 'As I daresay you can work out for yourself.'

The air in the room was warm and scented with something, a perfumed candle perhaps, or air freshener. Too sweet and sickly for Charmian's taste. She turned back to the photograph.

'Are you in it?'

Lou was pouring the coffee. 'No, not that group. I'm a year or two younger than Joan. We weren't that close as kids.'

'When I saw you together, I thought you were fond of each other.'

Lou nodded. 'Oddly enough, it grew with the years . . . of course, she could always explode. I mean, you saw that, accusing me of killing Diana – whom I didn't like I have to admit. She didn't mean it, it was one of her wild fits. To understand her, you have to accept that.'

Several dead girls had had to accept it too, Charmian thought.

'Our parents never could. Mum died before . . . well, before you know what, and Dad not long before, but he was always . . . well, tough on Joan, not so much with me. She wasn't loved.'

'Were you?'

'Not really, but I didn't mind.'

You always had a hard centre, which saw you through, thought Charmian. How odd, it's you that are the tough one, I can see that now, while Joan . . .

She gave up trying to assess Joan at that point.

'Is Rhos in the picture?'

Lou took her time filling a cup for Charmian, then carrying it across to her. 'Yes,' she said at last. 'Rhos is there. Would you like a biscuit?'

Charmian refused the biscuit as she drank her coffee. The only picture in the room, apart from the Constable reproduction, was that school picture.

Did that mean anything or nothing?'

'It was important to you,' she ventured.

Lou said without emotion that she supposed it had been. 'Outlived its time though now, I could throw it away.'

'Perhaps Joan would like it,' said Charmian. She picked it up for a closer look.

'Oh, I don't think so, in fact she suggested that I get rid of it.'

'I don't suppose I would want an old school portrait of myself around.' By picking up the photograph she had pulled it away from the green cardboard.

She saw that on the back of the photograph a schoolgirl scrawl read: Cathy Cathedral.

She raised an eyebrow at Lou. 'What does that mean?'

Lou shrugged and shook her head. 'No idea.'

'Someone tall with a pointed head,' suggested Charmian, with a laugh.

Lou did not join in the laugh.

'Could I keep this photograph?' asked Charmian. 'I'll give you a receipt, of course.'

'Why? Why should you want it?'

'Just for the record,' said Charmian.

Outside, with the photograph tucked away inside her big bag, Charmian wondered why she had been allowed to get away with it. She had an idea that Lou, just as clever in her own way as Joan, had been willing, even eager for her to take it away.

In the car she sat for a while studying it.

Cathy Cathedral, who are you?

There was a tall girl behind Rhos in the photograph, so perhaps this was the source of the joke.

She stowed the photograph away again, then looked up at the flat where Lou lived. There was Lou at the window looking down on her. With deliberation,

Charmian raised her hand to give a wave before she drove off. Lou did not wave back.

She opened the window as she drove, feeling the need to get the smell of that stuffy flat out of her nose and to let the air from the Great Park sweep in.

The dog, strolling insolently, tail aloft, through the Great Park was snuffing the sweet leafy air, to which he was indifferent, but he was picking up other, more animal, scents.

He had been moving steadily through the park for some time now and was perfectly happy. His search was going well. Not being a thinker, he did not have to ask himself why he was searching: it was just something dogs did, or his particular type of dog. Many generations back, there had been an Alsatian in his family tree and the gene for searching was still there. It was a pleasure to obey it.

He had two good smells to follow which seemed to run together, but he was concentrating on one, the other was an extra. He ploughed on. If a dog could be said to smile, he was smiling.

Ahead of him was a large expanse of water surrounded by trees. He was not a water lover himself, although of course he could swim. He slid into the lake, almost invisible now he was near to his goal. Instinct suggested he make himself unobtrusive.

He was seen however by another wanderer who wished to remain unnoticed.

Charlie Rattle had found himself a cosy nest in the trees and bushes where even the Rangers had not found him. He knew he could not stay for too long, food and drink were the problem, his supplies were limited. But for the moment, he was content to lie there, dry and warm. He had dreams about escaping to France or further afield still. He couldn't speak French but everyone spoke English, didn't they?

He did not think about what had happened to his mother in her own home, it was her own fault. Hardly anything to do with him at all. Uppermost in his mind, he felt cheerful and confident, but underneath he was frightened, very frightened.

From his hiding place, Charlie could see a couple sitting on the bank by the water, their backs towards him. He rested on his elbows, watching with interest.

What they were up to, if anything, he did not know. He was not an expert on sex. His own interest in it came and went. He did have a girlfriend who had promised to join him in France when he got there if he told her where to go and sent some money for a ticket. He couldn't see Marilyn in France somehow, so he didn't believe she would come, and certainly he would not be sending any money because he knew what she was like with money.

The dog was watching the scene too. He was behind Charlie, who did not know he was there. His interest was different: he knew one of the protagonists. In his wandering life he was a great picker-up of people whom he called friends. Sometimes they did not know they were friends and sometimes they became his enemies without knowing that either.

The dog watched as the couple by the waters stopped their conversation. He thought he heard the word 'No'. This prohibition was one he was familiar with. It didn't always stop him but he knew what the order was: a no was a no. And if you ignored it, a whack on the rump was likely to follow. Or the nose.

His nose twitched in memory.

He heard 'No', again. Not very loud, but he had big furry ears which heard splendidly.

He took a prudent step or two backwards. He knew a quarrel when he heard one.

Charlie who was watching also heard the protestation. The word had a special significance to him too. He wants sex and she's saying no, was his interpretation. It was a situation that he had met himself. He never pushed things, he didn't hold with violence to women. Not unless it was your mother, which you really could not be blamed for.

Then he saw the man raise his hand and deliver a chopping blow to the back of the woman's neck. She sagged against the man who gathered her up in his arms.

'Well, bugger me,' said Charlie to himself. He kept his eyes on the couple. Well, a look-see was on offer.

Then the man rolled the woman into the water, and sat there, watching.

Charlie frowned, wondering what to do.

The dog was watching too, He heard the splash of water. Saw a silver flash.

Sensibly, he turned and trotted off.

Chapter Eleven

Emily Agent rang Charmian at home with the news that Joan was lost while Charmian was considering whether to have an evening glass of wine, or get on with cooking the dinner first.

It was her turn to cook. If you could call it cooking. She contemplated the number of expensive, prepared meals in her freezer, then picked one out. Salad with it.

The dog watched her with interest, wondering what was coming his way.

'You look tired,' said Charmian kindly, as he sank back at full length while gently and slowly moving his tail. You could hardly call it a wag, more of a flop. It had been a long day for him.

'Oh, he's back, is he?' demanded Humphrey, entering the kitchen, with a bottle of wine and two glasses, 'been gone all day, the hound.' He added, 'Answer the phone, my hands are full.'

'Just his nature, he's a wanderer,' said Charmian, absently, as she reached out a hand for the telephone.

Emily handed over the news quickly and bleakly and then waited for the blast of anger that would greet her. Charmian did not disappoint her. When she was finished, Emily went on, 'We were at a lecture together and Joan left without my seeing.'

There was a bit of a defence: there had been slides, the room had been darkened, Joan had whispered that she would see better up in front, and had slid away through a door at the bottom of the room which Emily had not known about. Emily had shot out to find her and failed, gaining instead Inspector Parker's fury and Charmian's ice-cold anger.

'I've been out looking. Her sister thought she might have gone shopping. Apparently it's a sort of passion now she is able to get to the shops. She took plenty of money with her.' Emily explained to Charmian over the phone.

'You mean it was planned?'

'Yes, looks like it . . . I went in all the main stores, took another WPC with me. We went in all the washrooms. Inspector Parker alerted the uniformed branch, so they are looking for her, too. I must say, ma'am, that I thought she would turn up herself. Or that we would find her.'

'She could have gone to London.'

'We checked the trains, also the buses, and even taxis. Nothing. I think she is still in Windsor.'

The dog sank into a peaceful sleep, he knew a few answers to what was worrying them but passing them on was not what a dog did. He had smelt death in the Great Park and sensibly come home. To this home, anyway. It suited him at the moment, warmth, good food and no little children pestering him. People thought that dogs loved children: they did not, they put up with them. Dogs being natural actors and imitators could put up a good front.

'Right. I am going to call on Lou, you'd better meet me there.'

Humphrey watched her going, murmuring that he would be cooking the meal while she was out.

'Don't wait for me, eat when it's ready.' She kissed his cheek and grabbed her bag.

'Take the dog,' he yelled after her.

'No,' she called back.

Emily stepped out of her car as Charmian drove up to Lou's flat. 'She knows we're coming.'

Lou's flat smelt more stuffy than it had earlier as if no window had been opened nor anything cleaned for some time. She had known suspects smell like that under questioning. A concentration of worry, Charmian thought as she saw Lou.

Lou was edgy. 'Joan didn't say anything to me, just mentioned the lecture she was looking forward to and took her notes and then went off with Emily.'

'What about her son?'

'Pip? No, she wouldn't say anything to him. She was proud of him, and proud of the way he had stuck by her and not tried to change his identity, but she didn't talk to him much. They had nothing to talk about.'

Lou managed a smile for Emily, the two of them had become companionable, if not exactly friendly during the time that Joan had been living with her.

'She knew what she was going to do,' said Charmian, thinking of her flight down the darkened lecture hall towards the door hidden behind a curtain. 'She must have planned it.'

'I think she wanted a bit of freedom,' pleaded Lou, 'you can understand it after all those years inside . . . And she was more disturbed than she admitted about Diana being killed.'

'Why should that disturb her?'

'They knew each other a long while.'

'But they weren't friends.'

'No, not friends.'

'And they had quarrelled.'

'But Joan didn't kill Diana, she wasn't running away because of that.' Lou shook her head. 'She wasn't running away. All right, she had some plan, yes, but she knew she couldn't run anywhere.'

'Was she going to meet someone?' Charmian put the question she had been longing to ask.

Lou was silent for what seemed an eternity, blinking her eyes and not looking at Charmian and Emily. 'Yes, could be,' she said at last. 'That's why I didn't want to talk about it, if it's a friend she wanted kept out of things, which you can understand.'

Charmian nodded. Yes, she could understand.

'And if that's so, then she'll be back soon. She'll come walking through the door, any minute now. We only have to wait. She's going to be upset to find all of us here.'

'Who would that friend be?'

Lou shook her head. 'I don't know, don't know if there was one. Joan could be very close when she wanted to be.'

'She'd made friends with various people in prison . . . They came down here with her.'

'But they went back. They may have been in touch with her, she did have letters and phone calls, but I didn't listen in to her calls. I tell you, she hasn't gone off, she'll walk in any minute.'

Emily crouched in her corner and prayed that this would be so. She was in trouble, but it would be easier if Joan came back. They could share the complaining between them.

'I'm interested in that school photograph. Who do you think Cathy Cathedral was?' Charmian asked.

Lou shook her head. 'No idea, I've told you that already. It was a joke, I suppose. Or it might even have been her real name.'

'I don't think so.' Charmian stood up. 'Thank you for answering my questions.' Not that you've been any help, she managed to imply this in her tone. 'Let us know the minute Joan gets back.'

As they walked down the stairs, Charmian handed the school photograph over to Emily. 'Check with the school to see if they can identify Cathy Cathedral. She's the tall girl behind Joan and Rhos. It's a long while ago, but they may have a record. And take a note of the badges the girls are wearing. Remarkably like the cuts on both early and later murder victims.'

It rained hard that night. Emily was up early to go to the school that Rhos and Joan had attended to see if their records went back twenty odd years. It seemed doubtful, especially since the school was now subsumed into a great comprehensive, but she had to try.

She got nothing immediately but a promise that the secretary would look through the archives.

Meanwhile, Dolly Barstow and Rewley were going out looking for Joan Dingham. They were sharing a cup of coffee before starting for the day.

'She's definitely hopped it,' said Dolly.

'That would be so stupid.'

'Yes, but she'll have had a taste of freedom. She'll be

caught, of course she will, but I reckon she thinks it's worth the risk.'

It was Dolly who took the call from Inspector Parker who, in his turn, had been alerted to an incident by the park police.

A woman's body had been found in the lake. There was reason to believe it was Joan Dingham.

Suicide was suspected. There were attempts at suicide every so often, but usually they failed, because the police kept a careful watch. But a large lunch party with royalty present at one of the big houses in the park, together with a horse show, and the flowering of some special plants recently had strained the security forces, so this suicide had succeeded.

Dolly in her turn got in touch with Charmian.

'She's turned up. In the big lake. Drowned. Looks like suicide.'

The police surgeon, a quiet Scot called Dr Murdoch, the product of Edinburgh, was a careful, methodical man. At the end of his survey of the body, although certainly able to confirm she was dead, he had a problem.

Charmian got there quickly, in time to meet him before he left.

'Suicide?' she said.

He frowned. 'Not clear. There appears to have been a blow to the back of the head.'

Charmian was alert. 'Is that suspicious?' She knew it was, she just wanted him to put it plainly.

'She didn't kill herself,' he said bluntly. 'In my view, someone hit her on the back of the head and then dropped her in the water.'

'So it's murder.' A statement, not a question. It was similar to the way Rhos had died. 'Who had it in for Joan Dingham so badly that she had to be killed?'

'I'm only the police surgeon. The police pathologist will give you the official version.'

The area was ringed off, SOCO had arrived and the forensic team were at work.

'There are plenty of us here,' said Charmian, who was sitting on the grass with Dolly. She could see Inspector Parker and Emily Agent, and the local CID man, Inspector March. 'What's become of the band of friends and hangers-on that came south with Joan?'

'Been advised not to show their faces.'

Charmian nodded, as she looked at the police team.

'Let's leave them to it. I want to take the dog for a walk.'

Dolly was surprised, but she had learnt to take Charmian with calm.

'For some time,' Charmian said to Dolly, as she drove home. 'I have been wondering about Dr Harrie. I think he is worth pursuing.'

'Do you think he killed Joan?'

'He might have done . . . he's in there somewhere, I swear.'

'But not as Dr Harrie.'

'No, another face, another hat.'

Charlie Rattle watched the police activity from a discreet distance (although the word discretion was not in his personal dictionary), then withdrew further into the deep bushes. He had made a careful disposition of what he called his treasure and felt quite happy about that.

A high IQ is not necessary for the peace of mind of a killer. Might as well have a nap. He settled himself comfortably, unaware and uncaring of the activities of careful police searchers and forensic gleaners of evidence.

Charmian arrived to stop Humphrey in the drinking of his third cup of coffee – usually the best of the day.

'I want you to come with me, plus that dog, to the street where you said he lingered and wanted to go down and you wouldn't.'

Humphrey frowned. 'Don't know if I can remember where it was.'

'Come on, act like a dog, remember the way as you go.'

The dog, on the leash but charmingly eager, stepped out at a cracking pace. He led rather than was led, and was followed by Charmian and Dolly, with Humphrey holding the lead and protesting that he didn't quite believe in all this.

'Yes, it was near here,' said Humphrey as the dog sped through the neat, quiet back streets of Windsor. 'But we shall be in Old Windsor if he doesn't stop soon.' Breathlessly (he must remember to tell his doctor he could not walk so fast and get a check-up) he demanded of Charmian what she was up to. 'Solving several murder cases at once . . . Joke . . . I think the dog knows more than we do.'

'I wouldn't be surprised.' As they walked, Charmian told him that Joan Dingham was dead, probably murdered.

'Ah. And you are looking for Dr Harrie? You think the dog knows where he lives?'

'He might do, I hope so.'

'And you are putting together a picture?'

'I'm getting there,' said Charmian. 'Not crystal clear by any means.'

At the corner of Jackson Street, the dog paused, looked up at Humphrey and then walked on round the corner.

'I don't remember it being Jackson Street, but we might have approached it from the other side,' Humphrey said. They had been walking fast for about twenty minutes.

Halfway down Jackson Street a passage way led to a small row of houses, all neat and prosperous looking. A woman was in her front garden, trimming her roses. She looked at them with interest.

'Oh, there you are, Georgie,' she said to the dog. 'Haven't seen you for a while.'

The dog gave a quick bark and pressed on.

'He's going home, you see. Such a clever dog. I don't know if Mr Chappell's there though. I think he's out.'

'Which is Mr Chappell's house?'

The woman gave Charmian a doubtful look, but decided Humphrey at least looked respectable. She pointed. 'Next door but one, but the dog knows.'

The dog pushed open the gate and led them round the side of the house to the back door. Here he sat down and looked at them. He had done his bit, the rest was up to them.

'Mr Chappell,' said Charmian aloud. 'He's a craftsman and builder. He's done work for Baby's salon, she told me so, and I believe I saw him in the grounds around the block where Lou lives.'

'And you think he is Dr Harrie?'

In answer, Charmian hammered on the back door. 'You go and bang on the front door,' she told Dolly.

She could hear Dolly banging, but no one came, either to the back door or the front.

'I'd like to see inside,' said Charmian.

'I could break in.' Dolly was game. 'No problem.'

Charmian shook her head. 'Probably got an alarm system.'

Humphrey handed the dog's leash over to Charmian. 'Let an old soldier give you advice: always take the easy way out.'

He took the handle of the door, turned it and pushed. The door opened.

'It didn't look locked, somehow.'

The dog led the way in, found his water bowl and began to lap. Home, of a sort.

Charmian stood in the back hall which led to the kitchen.

'I'm going to have a look round. Humphrey, stay with the dog, Dolly come with me, and both of you forget this is happening.'

'I'd only do this for you,' said Dolly. 'If there's any trouble I will blame it all on you.'

Humphrey called to them. 'Look,' he was pointing at a row of hooks from which hung the usual raincoats and thick tweed overcoats, and next to them two wigs and one long hairy object. 'Dr Harrie. Wigs and a beard,' he said. 'Theatrical, isn't it?'

I always knew it would be, thought Charmian. The third type of killer, the theatrical type.

'Be quick,' Humphrey called after her as they went through the house. 'Something else I learnt in the army: be careful, be quiet and be quick.'

He could hear them moving about upstairs. It was to be hoped Mr Chappell did not come back. Then he heard them murmuring to each other. Come on, you two, he thought. There was a door in the back hall leading down to the basement, he had seen Charmian give it a look and he was afraid she might want to go down there.

They came down the stairs. 'All orderly and quiet up there,' said Charmian. 'But in a drawer in the desk, I found this.'

She held out a blue folder.

'Photographs . . . Let's go. You can look later.' Humphrey pleaded.

The woman had finished pruning her roses, but she watched them from the window and gave a wave.

Humphrey groaned. 'A witness . . . we shall all go to prison.'

'To prison, hell, in this folder I have evidence that this man was the third person in the early killings and that he killed the two later girls.'

'Why would he do that?'

'As a coming-home present for Joan.'

Dolly said nothing, she felt sick. She had seen the police photographs. There was one of Diana, too, her head hanging back and her eyes pushing out of her head after she was strangled.

In the Great Park, Joan's body had been taken away by the pathologist for examination. The forensic team were at work, inspecting the area around where Joan must have been rolled into the water. They found traces of her passage down the slope where she had rolled or been pushed. Traces of soil and vegetation, which would be checked, had been found on her clothes.

But to their surprise, they had found bloody traces on the grass and in the bushes. There was even a half-eaten hamburger as if someone had been sitting there. They had also found dog hairs. But it was the blood that interested them.

Joan had not bled. But someone else had done.

As soon as she could Charmian made her way to where Inspector March was installed in a police van which acted as a temporary incident room.

'I think I know who killed Joan,' she said quickly, handing over the blue folder. 'And I think he killed others as well. John Chappell.'

Inspector March listened gravely as he turned over the photographs in the folder. He had, of course, like Dolly, seen what official photographs there were but these were closer to the moment of approaching death, possibly taken while the victim was still alive. 'Nasty,' he said. 'At least he didn't use a video as well like that American killer.'

'He's the killer.'

March nodded. 'You could be right . . . Only thing is, someone has killed him.'

They had searched the bushes, following the trail of blood.

Hidden in a thicket was the body, folded up neatly on itself like an embryo.

'It's John Chappell all right, he had identification on him,' he went on, 'Dr Murdock had a good look at him, examined him with care. He died from several stab wounds.'

'Yes, good.'

'The only other thing is: he's not a man, he's a woman.'

'Cathy Cathedral,' said Charmian, when she had collected her thoughts. 'It was a joke, she was a tall, hefty girl, probably boyish and she got that nickname. Catherine Chappell. She'll be in the school records.'

She sat in the temporary incident room talking things over with Inspector March.

'I am sure he killed Joan. She wanted to be free, and he wanted to hang on to her. She was frightened of him, I think, as Rhos had been. He must always have been the prime mover in those early murders. He was a theatrical murderer with a strong sense of drama. I am going to go on saying him not her . . . he had built himself up so successfully as John Chappell, builder. But who killed him?'

'The stab wounds,' said Rewley from a spot by the door where he had managed to find room, 'don't they suggest something to you? If I had to make a guess I'd say Charlie Rattle. He's on the loose with a knife and he's a man who enjoys using it.'

'Does he have a dog?' asked March, looking at the forensic notes. 'One with rough brown hair?'

'No,' said Charmian, 'but Chappell did, and I think the dog may have been out looking for him.'

'If you are looking for Charlie,' said Rewley, 'perhaps we should get the dog.'

But there was no need. Charlie was found by a park ranger who could hear his snores coming out of the bushes where he was asleep.

Lou and Pip were told about Joan's death and Pip went to the mortuary to identify her.

'Yes, that's Mum. I never knew her well, but she was good to me.'

Pip was asked if his father was still alive and said that he had no idea, he had left the scene a long while ago, for which Pip did not blame him. Yes, he would see to the death announcement and to the funeral once the coroner released the body.

Lou and Pip went home together.

Charmian told Baby that she thought that Diana's killer had been found dead himself. She told her briefly what it seemed right she should know.

Baby listened. 'I think Diana and her book must have seemed a threat to Chappell. And of course, he had done so much work for me that he knew his way in and out of my place.' She gave a shiver. 'Nasty. He might have got me too.'

'I shouldn't worry about that.'

'No. I won't.' Baby was always practical. 'But the sad thing is, I don't believe Diana would have written that book. She was going to die anyway. She was playing a game like she did sometimes. Now Lou will write the book. He ought to have gone after Lou.'

'He might have done, if he hadn't got killed first.'

Hard to think of Charlie Rattle as a good angel, but perhaps they came in odd packets.

'That's the end of the bodies,' one of the police team said to Charmian. 'Not a bad total.'

To Inspector March, she said that she wanted a thorough inspection of Chappell's house. 'We may find relics and evidence relating to the earlier crimes. He lived here then, it was his – her parents' house, he was at college in London, already working on a building course. He may have done some practical work here.'

'What do you mean?' asked the alert Inspector March.

'Just thinking.'

'Naturally we will be making a survey of the house. We might find his camera.'

Down the basement stair was a wine cellar and a coal cellar with an old furnace. The floor had been covered with paving stones of some antiquity, but an area had been disturbed.

Charmian looked at Inspector March who nodded at the team working with him. 'Dig it up,' he ordered.

Not far down, but neatly disposed of were the skeletal remains of a man.

'I am only guessing,' said Charmian, 'but I would say this is Joan Dingham's husband, of whom Chappell must have been bitterly jealous. I think Mr Dingham was the first victim of all, and that as a result of the pleasure Chappell got from this killing all the rest followed. This chap was Act One.'

He was the theatrical type of killer, she thought,

and Charlie Rattle the disorganized sort. Perhaps it was poetic justice.

Charmian and her team had dinner together the day after the coroner's inquests on Joan Dingham and John Chappell. Two inquests on the same day. The inquest on Edward Dingham had yet to be held.

But the three of them felt that they could now draw the curtain.

Emily Agent had come up to Charmian at the inquest on Chappell. 'I didn't go on with the hunt for Cathy Cathedral, there didn't seem much point. But I did manage to get in touch with one of the retired teachers who remembered all three girls. It seems they were all expelled – not that that word was used – asked to leave was the way it was put. They were, well, victimizing younger girls, if I can put it that way. The teacher was cagey but she got across that selected young girls were being initiated into sexual behaviour too advanced for their years. They had signs similar to the school badge scratched into their arms. They got chucked out when it was discovered.

'Lou never said.'

'No, she wouldn't, but she must have known. She wasn't mixed up in it, though. I guess that was when it all started, ending up in murder. I suppose Chappell was the initiator. Amazing how the other two protected him – her.'

'Thanks for telling me. And I suppose we will never know what set Chappell off.'

'Parents usually get the blame somehow, but I don't know.'

'No. Would you like to eat with us tonight?'

'No, I'm off out. Guess what? The Greenhams have asked me to a party.'

Keep your distance from the good doctor, Charmian wanted to warn but didn't. Emily could look after herself.

Charmian served the meal to her friends with relief at being off the hook.

They ate salmon and salad and drank white wine which Humphrey poured. The dog ate salmon too.

'I suppose we've got him for life,' said Charmian, for the second time since his arrival.

'I don't know.' Humphrey was doubtful. 'He still wanders off you know. He's not always with us.'

The telephone rang while they were drinking coffee. Charmian took the call.

A soft pleasant woman's voice spoke, 'I'm sorry to bother you,' she said. 'And do forgive me if I've got it wrong . . . But I saw a picture in the local paper of you with a dog and it looked so like our Pete that I wondered if it could be. Have you had him long?'

'No, not very long,' said Charmian looked down at the dog, lying at her feet. 'Yes. I reckon he could be your Pete . . . he's smallish but strong with shaggy light brown fur.'

'It does sound like Pete,' she gave a light laugh. 'He is a wanderer. We call him the dog with three homes.'

Could be, thought Charmian. Or four or five. I reckon he likes to change as it suits him.

'But the children do love him and they miss him so much. And he loves them, of course. Could I come and collect him?'

'Yes, do.' And she told the caller her address. Then

she turned to the rest of them. 'Well, you all heard that: he's off home where the children all miss him so much.'

Very soon a battered Land Rover drove up, and Pete was led to the door. Four lively children, two boys and two girls, hurled themselves at him with cries of joy. Their pretty young mother thanked Charmian for her great kindness to the dog.

'He is such a nice dog, but an innocent really.'

Oh, yes, thought Charmian, an innocent who's probably watched at least one murder and maybe a couple of others. He probably helped in the invention of the hermit and Dr Harrie. Birdie was the wise one, she was always cautious with him.

She waved Pete goodbye as he was deposited in the Land Rover with the children. She saw that he had his jaws firmly fixed round the china hand which he had stolen from Baby. His toy.

As they drove off, it seemed to Humphrey that Pete gave him a straight look.

You haven't seen the last of me, the look said. I'll be back. I'm not staying with this lot, I don't like children.